BED
OF
ROSES

BED OF ROSES

A NOVEL

CAYLEE HAMMACK
&
CAROLYN BROWN

Podium

Cover design by Dawn Adams

ISBN: 979-8-3470-0766-0

Published in 2025 by Podium Publishing
www.podiumentertainment.com

Podium

To the mother & aunt who encouraged me to read.
To the best friend who inspired me to write.
To the man who taught me what good love is.
To the author who helped me bring this world to life.
To the human reading this now.

If it wasn't for you, this piece of work would not exist.
Thank you.

FOREWORD

I believe that we get the ability to speak life into our dreams, and I do so often, with anything and everything. One day, I plan to walk a section of the Great Wall of China just to see how far I can get in a day. When I'm an old lady, I'm going to get my wildlife rehabilitation license and raise and release the hurt critters I find. I also have musical goals that I fixate on from time to time. I listened to an interview with Ray Charles a while back, then saw a picture of him on the stage at Carnegie Hall. Now, I'm going to play Carnegie Hall—it's been decided. I'm going to send up a prayer that the Lord will ask Ray to be on that stage with me when I do. These are aspirations that I hold no superstitions about. But there are some dreams I hold close to my chest and lock into the gun safe when guests come over. I whisper to them, and I pray they come true, but I rarely share them. I'm too afraid of the world ripping them apart before they've had a chance to grow—before I can do right by them and give them good legs to stand on.

Writing a book and seeing it come to fruition seemed like the most vivid fever dream; always just out of reach, on the fringe of reality. I attempted writing my first fantasy story when

I was thirteen. Then at fifteen, I left that idea to rot and started working on another, which was fueled by a discovery of Bram Stoker and two of the Brontë sisters. I got to page seventy-three before it died, alongside the other story, in the hospice section of my computer folders, forever entombed on my first laptop that hasn't powered on in years. In quiet moments while writing this book, I have sensed that younger version of myself step in and guide my hands. It's as if some creative hibernation has ended within me, and roses now grow where I thought only stones lay.

There's a peach tree in my front yard; I can see it through the window from where I sit and write. In 2019, my parents brought cartons of Elberta peaches up from Georgia for my Grand Ole Opry debut. My dad left one of the peach pits in my sink. I took the pliers he gave me and cracked it open, determined to grow my own here in Nashville. I put the soft kernel and some damp sand in a plastic bag and tucked it into my refrigerator door—just as the instructions online said to—then I forgot all about it. Months later, before heading out on tour, I was deep cleaning and found the little baggy. It was swollen with pale green leaves curling into themselves in the sand. A peach tree had sprouted right under my nose, in my very own kitchen. That tree now stands in my yard. Timing is everything. Patience has led to secret childhood dreams come true, in peaches and in this book.

The musical garden of songs on the *Bed of Roses* album and the small town square of Homestead in this book are meant to go hand-in-hand, for one is the child of the other. If I hadn't created the album, I never would have created this book. If Carolyn and I had never collaborated, it would've left a whole array of backstories behind this album unexplored. More than anything, I wanted to write this story to create a world that you can retreat to when you need to feel good. I have used books and music as escapes since childhood; as manuals and tools; as reminders that happily-ever-afters do exist. Use this book and my music however you need to. May they do well by you when you need them most.

C. H.

BED
OF
ROSES

CHAPTER ONE

TUMBLEWEED MEN

Y ou won't make it five miles past the Rosepine City Limits sign in that rattletrap of a car, Sambo," her father's voice echoed in her head.

"You are wrong, wrong, wrong," she singsonged to the dash.

Her dog, Nibbler, threw back his head and howled from the patched passenger seat of her 1965 Mustang. Sam wasn't quite sure whether his vocal performance proved that he loved or hated Bob Dylan, but the proud stance he took near the cracked window for this impromptu concerto made her laugh. His tail wagged almost in time, and he looked like he was smiling any time she looked over at him. Yes, ma'am, this trip was exactly what they both needed.

"It's a bonafide fact, Nibs. The older the violin"—she patted the dashboard—"the sweeter the music. Patsy is going to take us to Mena, Arkansas, without a single hiccup. Besides, I'm grown." Thirty came with a resounding need to be able to stand on her own two feet, so this trip was going to be a conquest. "I can take care of myself. I can take care of you too if you want, critter."

Nibbler agreed with a short bark.

She had almost convinced herself that the first rattle the car had made was caused by a stray tumbleweed she had run over a few minutes before. The second mechanical shudder had her eyeing the rearview mirror, hoping to see the culprit launch away behind them. She accidentally hit a big pothole, and for a few seconds, the jarring sound that had set in went away miraculously.

When gray smoke started to ooze from the side panels of the car's hood, she glanced over at Nibbler with the same puzzled look he sported. "Maybe it's just burning something off. I bet it's burning that tumbleweed off and it'll stop any minute now."

She had only gone a hundred yards past the last speed limit sign when the rattle turned into a thumping noise and black smoke began to billow from under the car's hood.

"Well, shit!" She scrambled as she opened the door, got out, and took in the scene. She opened the hood, and a cloud of nasty-smelling smoke swamped her before it dissipated among the branches of the tall pines.

She coughed several times and stumbled back, waving the smoke away best she could. This wasn't in the plans. Her daddy was gonna give her so much hell for this—oh, so much hell. She hollered for Nibbler to load out. He hopped out of the car and trotted up to sit beside her, head cocked a bit as if assessing the situation.

It took a minute to swallow her pride before she rounded the edge of the vehicle and retrieved her phone from the passenger seat. She hated eating crow, but she didn't know a soul in this area, and whether she'd like to admit it or not, she needed help. The only option she had was to call her father. As slow as traffic was in that area, she could be sitting in her car all night waiting for him to come get her.

She climbed into the driver's seat and inhaled deeply, let her breath out slowly, then felt her phone slip from her trembling hands. It scooted across the floor like it had been greased and flew under the driver's seat. She bent over the wheel, and her long wavy red hair cascaded into her face. She pushed it back several times, but it fell forward every time she tried to retrieve her phone. Finally, she twisted it all up into a messy bun and held it there with a clamp she had stuck on the visor.

"I might as well be working blind," she grumbled when she couldn't get a firm grasp on the phone. By stretching her fingers, she finally touched the edge and slowly pulled it toward her—inch by inch—until she had it in her hands.

"Victory!" she shouted as she stood up and out of the car and joined Nibbler, who was waiting patiently for her.

The sound of a vehicle approaching gave her hope that some farmer or maybe a Good Samaritan would stop, work a little magic, and she would be on her way within a few minutes. But if anything, the pickup truck sped up when the driver saw her stranded car.

"This is hostile territory, Nibbler. If we were back in Rosepine, someone would have already stopped to help us. I'm glad we don't live anywhere near here," she grumbled.

Then why did you leave? Her mother Wanette's voice popped into her head.

Nervousness had seeped into Sam's thoughts when the smoke appeared. And wariness was stepping in now as the smoke slowed, but the car didn't stop cranking. Plus, her mother's voice in her head was getting louder.

She wasn't in the mood to argue with her mama, not in her head and not on the phone right now. Especially not when she had to call her father and listen to the fresh batch of I-told-you-sos he'd whip up. He had warned her about the Mustang, about driving it long distances, hell, about buying it in the first place.

"I ain't gonna break down anywhere. Besides, you taught me how to protect myself," she had chirped back at him. What *a little hypocrite I am now*, she thought, *scared and stranded in the badlands of the Bible Belt. If only knowing self-defense was as good for emotional defense as it was for physical.* But then Nibbler sneezed and snapped her out of her inner monologue of pity.

She stared at her phone in her hand for a minute as Nibbler went about his own business, his aim seemed to be marking every tire of the car. The woods were thick around them, reminding her of the survival shows she used to watch with her ex. Bears could be found in woods like this, at least on that show they watched that was based in Nova Scotia. Texas woods couldn't be much different, she suspected. She put the leash back on Nibbler and explained to the displeased dog that it was for his own safety.

Two more vehicles passed her by before she pulled the trigger and finally, with a long sigh, scrolled down to her father's phone number and hit the call button. CALL FAILED popped up, and the Irish temper passed down on her mama's side rose from the depths of her soul. If she had to pay a dollar for every cuss word that flowed from her mouth, the gallon-sized cuss jar sitting on the kitchen cabinet at her mama's would be overflowing by now.

Like most folks, she had relied on GPS for directions, but no cell service meant she had lost that luxury too. Her father had advised her to take his old atlas with her, but she was far too hard-headed for that. She had GPS. She would keep her phone charged. She would be fine.

"Dammit!" she swore again when she remembered that she had been listening to her driving playlist, and streaming music was probably the battery-sucking culprit. Her vintage car offered a cigarette lighter, but no charging plug-in, and it hadn't worked since she had bought it. Now stranded with three percent battery life left, the reality of just how hellishly inconvenient that broken cigarette lighter was suddenly became clear. She closed her eyes tightly and tried to remember what the tinny voice of the GPS lady had last said.

"I'm supposed to stay on Highway 59 for one hundred and forty-six miles," she whispered and groaned. What if there were no more towns between here and Mena, Arkansas? She'd planned on getting to her cousin's house tonight, seeing her off, and house-sitting till she got back. Now, it was looking like Sam might not make it to Mena 'til God knows when. The longer Sam stared out at the pine-spotted woods, the more she thought about bears. Maybe her dad should've taught her wilderness training instead of hand-to-hand sparring. A book in her duffel bag collection in the back seat titled *How to Stay Alive in the Woods* could really come in handy.

When she had stopped back about an hour ago, she remembered that Nibbler had hiked his leg on a wooden sign for a bed-and-breakfast called Rose Garden in the historic town of Homestead.

"I wonder how far that place is?" The wind didn't answer but instead blew a couple of tumbleweeds, Nibbler's new favorite adversary, onto the road's shoulder. He snapped out at the closest one, like a furry little crocodile, and just missed.

"You might be small, but you are vicious." She patted him on his head. "If a couple bears are hiding behind those tall pine trees, they better think twice about coming out here, huh?" As if he understood her, he took up a guard position—his head held high, his small body tense.

"It's kinda funny seeing two tumbleweeds just roaming around with this many trees. Out here in a land of trees, tumbleweeds are as out of place as we are," she said aloud to her surroundings, and it felt like the woods swallowed her words up.

Sam tugged on his leash. "I appreciate the security detail, Nibs, but we have got to start walking. It will be dark in another hour."

She locked the driver's door and took a couple of steps when Nibbler growled and focused on the road ahead of them. Another vehicle was coming around the curve a few yards away, and hope rose in her when the big truck slowed to a stop beside her car. Maybe there were decent people in this part of the world after all.

A tall, lanky guy with thick dark hair and catlike green eyes opened the door and stepped out onto the road. "Looks like you need some help. I'm Jack Reynolds from down in Homestead. I own the nearest auto shop and towing business—actually the only one in the county." He jerked his thumb back to the sign on the side of the truck but kept his eyes on Sam. "Want a ride into town where I can take a look at what's going on under the hood of this pretty thing?"

Anyone who complimented Patsy couldn't be all bad, even if he was wearing a Dallas Cowboys T-shirt.

"Yes, please," Sam said, but Nibbler continued a low, droning growl at her feet. "How long will it take to fix it, ya think?"

Jack's crystal clear green eyes raked over her like a starving man would look at a plate of fried chicken. Her gut might have been wrong about Patsy holding together long enough to get her to Mena, but she'd bet dollars to cow patties that she was standing in front of a prime example of what her memaw would've called a rake.

"Now, darlin'," he drawled and flashed a brilliant smile, "that's a question I can't answer until I take it back to my shop and take a good look at it, but I can't get it done today, and it probably won't be ready to go for two or three days. Parts for a vintage car like this ain't easy to find. Good things take a little time." He smiled and winked at her.

Even blindfolded and half lit, Sam could smell a man like him coming from a mile away. Her ex had the same sort of piercing green eyes that could be so boyish and yet devilish at the same time. Today, she was in no mood for flirting or falling for whatever other moves he had probably perfected. All she needed was a ride to town, a little cell service, and everything would be just fine. Her dad would bring his truck and tow her over to Mena. He would help her find a mechanic who could fix Patsy, and bam, life would go on.

"Let's just get on with this," she grumbled as she picked up her dog and crawled up into the passenger seat of the truck while he loaded Patsy.

She mentally thumbed through the money in her bank account. She had enough in her savings to get her by for a few days—a few weeks if she was frugal—but then the cost of repairs to Patsy had to be added in too. Tallying up her dismal-looking mental checkbook put that little voice in her head—the one that told her she must prove to her father and to herself that she could be completely independent and be fine on her own—the one starting to wail for her attention again.

For a while, after the big betrayal of her best friend and boy-friend of three years, she had lost all her confidence. Then the offer came from her cousin to get away from Rosepine, and Sam had agreed instantly, thinking it might give her heart some reprieve. If she went anywhere in her hometown, it seemed just like fate that she would run into Chase or Liza Beth. She couldn't escape what had happened if she stayed in Rosepine. Earlier that day, when her hometown disappeared in her cracked rearview mirror, she felt like a clean slate appeared ahead of her. Her confidence seemed to be waking up, and she wasn't going to lose ground now.

When Chase and Sam had broken up the first time, her elderly friend Inez had poured her a double and told her that everything happened for a reason, and sometimes when you walk through pain, you find joy on the other side. How she wished Inez were here now to coach her through this situation. Sam wondered what her wise old friend would do if she were in her shoes.

"All done and ready to rock and roll," Jack said as he slid in behind the steering wheel and gave Sam another of those hungry looks. "Where are you coming from and where are you headed, pretty lady?" He checked all the mirrors and then pulled out onto the road.

At least he was a careful driver, her brain pointed out. Nibbler ducked his head down and growled—low and down deep—as if telling Sam in the ways that only a dog can that this fella wasn't to be trusted. He had never liked Chase either. That old saying about dogs being a good judge of character came to mind, and she vowed that from now on, she would listen to her dog.

Noted, Nibbler.

"Are you going to answer me?" Jack asked with a bit of edge to his voice. "And shut that ugly mutt of yours up or—"

"Or what?" she snapped, cutting him off.

Jack chuckled. "Whoa there, you got a little fire to go with all that red hair. I like that in a woman."

"Is that really a pickup line? If so, don't even waste your breath. I was on my way to Mena, Arkansas, and I was coming from Rosepine, Louisiana. Did someone in one of the cars that passed by me call you?"

No, ma'am. I was on my way home from delivering a pickup truck to Linden when I saw your smoke signal. I followed it and found you. We don't have a motel or anything in Homestead, but I've got an apartment above my auto shop that I'll gladly share with you 'til we get you back up and running. It may take a while." Jack smiled and turned his feline green eyes over at Sam to see her reaction.

Bad boy to the bone marrow, Sam thought.

"Firstly, I don't even know you, and secondly, I'm not that kind of girl. Thirdly, I think you're pulling my leg. What about the bed-and-breakfast?" She pointed to the Rose Garden sign they were driving past.

"Yeah, the Rose Garden. It's the only place in town where you can stay if you turn down my offer," he answered and glanced over at her again. "Honey, you can't blame a man for trying. I've always had a soft spot in my heart for redheads, especially those with pretty blue eyes."

Sam bit back a retort, figuring she had tested her good graces with God and the universe enough for one day. "Who runs the Rose Garden?"

"Ole Kathleen Scott owns the B&B and the Rose Petal Flower Shop. She is a salty old gal, and nothing gets past her. She's also the mayor of Homestead and president of the chamber of commerce here. She's just a big fish in a little pond, but most everyone thinks she hung the moon."

The edge in his voice made Sam suspect that Jack must have had a run-in or two with Ms. Scott.

"Good to know," Sam muttered and flipped Nibbler around to face the door in hopes that he would stop growling. "Are there any other towns between here and Mena?"

"Nope, and nothing in any direction for a few miles," Jack answered. "Jefferson is down south. Linden is north. Homestead was built years ago near the Scotts Bayou. Old-timers who come in the shop go on and on about when their great-grandpas had cotton fields, and they'd shipped the bales down the bayou to Jefferson. That was back before the timber companies bought up all the land to grow pine."

"Scotts Bayou," I repeated. "Does that have anything to do with Kathleen Scott?"

"She claims that it does, but she also says that her ancestors came over here from Scotland. Who knows with that old coot." He smiled over at her. "Enough of the history lesson. Let's talk about you. You didn't tell me whatcha name was?"

"I'm Samantha, this here is Nibbler."

"He's one ugly little mutt. Is he a Heinz?" Jack chuckled.

"No, he's part poodle mix and part immaculate conception. Mama's dog sneaked out of the backyard one night, and sixty days later she had just one pup, Nibbler. Daddy said I could keep him because he said he'd"—she covered the dog's ears with her hands and whispered—"die of ugly by the time he was six weeks old. But just so you know . . ." She shot a dose of stink eye to Jack. "I don't take too kindly to folks using that language when they talk about him."

"My apologies," Jack said with another chuckle.

"What is a Heinz?" she asked.

"Like the ketchup—fifty-seven varieties," he answered.

Sam smiled despite her attempt to bite it back. "From now on, I will tell anyone who asks that he is purebred Heinz and that his ancestors are of a rare breed from Germany."

"Where they bred the dogs to keep the foxes out of the tomato fields, right?"

Sam liked a man with a sense of humor, and she remembered something her memaw told her when she had started dating Chase and thought he had a halo floating above his perfectly styled hair.

"Be careful," Memaw had said, "there's good and bad in

everyone on the face of the earth. If a person was all bad, then the devil would jerk 'em straight down to hell. If they were all good, they'd bypass this life and go straight to heaven."

"Did I get it wrong?" Jack asked. "Maybe the dogs kept gophers out of the onion fields."

"I'm not sure which one," she played along, "but I can assure you that the breed would keep varmints out of the crops, both the four-legged and two-legged varieties. The breed is also a good judge of character, I hear." She shot a pointed look toward him.

"Talk some more," Jack said. "I like your accent."

"What do you want me to talk about?" she asked.

"Anything. Tell me about Rosepark."

"Do you mean Rosepine?" she asked.

"Whatever that town is you came from. Tell me why you left it?"

"Rosepine is a small town with less than two thousand people. Everyone knows everybody in town by name. Everybody knows what everyone else is doing, when they did it, and who they did it with, and then they read the weekly parish newspaper to see who got caught. The reason I left is classified. I could tell you, but then I'd have to kill you," Sam answered.

"That's fine. I'm a pretty good detective," Jack declared. "I bet you recently got out of a bad relationship."

Sam used a lot of willpower to keep from gasping. "Why would you think that?"

"A gorgeous woman like you wouldn't be driving a piece of junk car such a long distance if she wasn't running away from someone. Were you married, and the sorry bastard that did you wrong kept the good vehicle in the divorce?" he asked.

"I'm not divorced," Sam answered. "And I don't like for people to call Patsy a junk car any more than I like for anyone to say my dog is"—she covered his ears again—"ugly. And it could be that I'm running toward something instead of getting away from someone."

The noise of a rooster crowing right beside her startled Sam. She glanced out the window, but no chickens anywhere out there. Then she traced the sound to a phone lying on the console between them. The name Kara flashed above a picture of a scantily dressed, blond-haired woman in a sexy pose. Then a text message appeared that said *Same time tonight?*

Jack grabbed the phone, hit a button, and shoved it into his shirt pocket. "I can't go anywhere without Buster—that's my mechanic at the stop—calling to see when I'll be back. Where were we? Oh, yes, you are married but not divorced. Honey, I'm good with that."

Lord have mercy! He wasn't only a bad boy; he was a pushy one. He had a woman named Kara who must have seen him last night and wanted to see him again, and he was flirting big-time with Sam. She wondered how many women's numbers were stored in his phone, and if he lied to all of them. Poor Kara was headed up shit creek without a paddle if she thought this guy could be trusted.

I'll only be in Homestead until my car gets fixed, she told herself, *and then I'll be on my way. So, whatever Kara or Jack do is none of my concern. Which reminds me, I need to call Greta and tell her that I won't be in Mena for a few days.* Samantha reached into her hip pocket and pulled out her phone.

"Cell service is spotty up in these woods," Jack said. "I have no idea how Buster got through with that call a few minutes ago."

Sam looked down at her phone and shivered when she found that the battery was now completely dead. The cord to recharge it was in one of her bags in the trunk of her car, and even though Jack seemed harmless—except for those leering looks and his incessant flirting—she still wondered if she had trusted him too much.

Maybe she should have asked to use his phone to call home and wait for her father.

"Got a problem?" Jack asked.

"My phone is dead. I keep in touch with my mama when I'm on the road. She and my dad will be worried if I don't check in every couple of hours," Sam explained, hoping that if she had gotten in the truck with a serial killer, that would deter him.

You've been watching too many cop shows. Her mother's voice was back in her head.

Probably so, she agreed inwardly.

She sure was glad when she saw a faded sign along the side of the road that said "The Second Baptist Church welcomes you to Homestead."

There it was written down for all the world to see, and her phone was dead as a railroad spike, so she couldn't take a picture to prove it to her dad. When they had taken road trips and passed so many First Baptist church signs welcoming folks to whatever town they were about to go through, he would chuckle and ask just where the Second Baptist church was located.

The next sign said "Scottie's Bar and Grill: Where everyone knows your name."

Dad would love this place, she thought. He always said that all a community needed to be a real town was a church and a watering hole. According to him, folks had to have a place to sow their wild oats on Saturday night and a place to pray for a crop failure on Sunday morning.

"Isn't that business about everyone knowing your name a copyright infringement?" Sam wanted to talk about something else. She would remember the fun she had with her father later, after he raked her over the coals for not listening to him.

"Who knows?" Jack shrugged. "Could be that the television

show from all those years ago got the motto from Scottie instead of the other way around."

"Looks like the type of town where everyone knows everything about everyone, not just their name," Sam mused.

"Pretty much." Jack slowed down when he passed the city limits sign.

"Kathleen Scott, Scotts Bayou, and Scottie's Bar. I'm surprised the town isn't named Scottsville," Sam said, trying to keep the conversation away from herself.

"It was named Homestead because the first settlers that came to the area found the remnants of an old log cabin with flowers blooming all around it. When there were enough people to have a post office, they needed a name for the town. The wife of the first family of settlers had begun to tell people that they had built their home just past the old homestead, so that's what they chose," Jack said.

"Do you give guided history tours for all of the tourists who come through?" she quipped, bemused.

"For the pretty ones, I do, and the tour is free of charge." He winked over at her again. "That's just what I've been told anyway. Who knows if it's true."

By the time she had come up with a witty enough response to bite back at his flirtation, she noticed a big two-story house sitting on a hill behind a clearing of thin white pines. "Wait! Is that the B&B?"

"Yeah, it is," he answered. "I don't want to drive up that narrow lane with a car behind me. I'd have a devil of a time backing out."

She saw a couple convenience stores, a florist, a post office, and then a few more storefronts down, a bookstore named Everbloom caught her eye. "Why would someone name a bookstore that?"

"Beats me. Noah Carter owns that place. He's always been a

strange bird. In high school, he never played any sports. With his size and build, he would have made a great football player, but he had his nose stuck in a book all the time. He was one of *those kids*." Jack emphasized the last two words with air quotes, then quickly put his hands back on the steering wheel.

Sam would go to war with anyone who called Patsy a piece of junk. She was of the same frame of mind about Nibbler being referred to as ugly. But what really riled her up was bullies who looked down on people who were a little different and didn't have the same set of social rules. She didn't know Noah, but if he followed his dream by being surrounded by books, then she could appreciate him.

"Got to say though," Jack went on as he drove past several houses, "if I had Noah's money and Laura to hug up next to at night, I might do something silly like put in a bookstore. I heard that books draw women like flies, but Noah wouldn't know about that. Once a nerd, always a nerd. I don't know what Laura sees in him, other than he's as rich as Midas."

"Who is Laura?"

"Just the prettiest woman in Homestead," Jack said with a hint of sadness, but then his expression and tone changed. "At least until I picked you up on the side of the road. Now you have the crown." A chronic flirt—that was Jack in a nutshell.

"And Noah is married to her?" Sam asked.

"No, he's been dating her for around two years, I reckon. One of these days, he's gotta get up the nerve to ask her to marry him. She is as impatient as she is easy to look at, so I'm betting that if he doesn't pull that trigger soon, she's bound to jump a fence to greener pastures. Everyone in town thinks she's hanging on for a ring so she's got a shot at all his money. He inherited a virtual gold mine from his grandpa when the old man died."

Jack braked and parked Patsy into a bay in a garage with a big sign above the doors. "Jack's Auto Shop. If your vehicle needs it, we do it."

"There's gold back here among all the trees?" Sam asked.

"Nope. I said virtual gold," Jack replied. "His ancestors made a mint in agriculture years and years ago, and then his grandpa invested in oil. We're here. Let's pop the hood of your car and see what Buster thinks is wrong."

Sam opened the truck door, got out, and set Nibbler on the ground. He did his due diligence, promptly marking the tire of the tow truck as his territory and kicked gravel up on it after he was done. The shop smelled like a mixture of stale coffee, old motor oil, and sweat.

"Hey, Jack!" A big guy with a round face and bald head came from between the vehicles in the other two bays and kneeled in front of Nibbler. "What's your name, cutie?"

Nibbler licked his outstretched hand and wagged his tail. Evidently, Buster could be trusted if that old saying about dogs and kids having a sixth sense was true.

"His name is Nibbler," Sam answered.

"Well, if you ever get tired of him, give me a call. I love animals," Buster said and straightened up. "My wife, Allie, would love to have another pup in the house."

"Not a chance," Sam said with a smile.

"Well, hot damn!" Buster said when he saw Patsy roll off the trailer. "I haven't seen one of those in years. What's the matter with her?"

"Enough to keep ya busy, I reckon. Buster, meet Samantha," Jack said as he came around the side of the Mustang. "Samantha, this is Buster, my partner in the business."

"Jack fetches them and does oil changes and takes care of

tires. I fix the major stuff," Buster explained as he straightened up. "Let's see what's going on under the hood of this pretty little thing."

Sam wondered why the place wasn't named Buster's Auto Shop, or at the very least, Buster and Jack's, but she didn't ask.

Jack opened the hood and stood to the side. "Samantha was on her way up to Mena when her car started blowing black smoke. I figure it's the head gaskets. What do you think?"

Buster shook his head slowly the whole time he checked things out. "Ms. Samantha, this is a vintage car, but my first thought is that it's going to take way more to cure her than she's worth. I'll clean up all the smoke damage tomorrow morning, and then I'll know more. All the junkyards in this part of the state are closed for the day, and that's where I'd have to scavenge for parts. I've got a date with my wife in half an hour anyhow, so I need to leave and get cleaned up." He handed her a small notebook. "Write down your cell number, and I'll call you soon as I know something. Sound good?"

"Sounds as good as I'll get. I'll be at the Rose Garden if there's room," Sam answered and scribbled down her number.

"The good news is that there will be room. Ms. Kathleen brought her Caddy in yesterday for an oil change and said that business had been slow all winter, but now that spring is here, she's hoping it will pick back up."

Buster headed to the back of the shop, and then Sam heard a door slam and the engine of a truck starting up.

"Alone at last," Jack said with a twinkle in his green eyes. "I will take the price of the tow job off your bill if you'll have a burger and a beer with me at Scottie's. You can use my phone to call the bed-and-breakfast, and I'll drive you up there before midnight.

Wouldn't want my truck to turn into a pumpkin."

"I would appreciate a ride, but I'm tired and I'm sure Kathleen, or maybe I should call her Mrs. Scott, would rather I check in earlier than midnight," Sam retorted.

Jack's phone rang, and this time he smiled when he looked at the screen. Sam wasn't being nosy but from where she stood, she could see that it was the same Kara who had texted him earlier. He walked away and whispered through the conversation. When he finished, he came back to where she and Nibbler were standing beside Patsy.

"I'm sorry, but I have to take care of some business. The B&B is not far. Remember we passed by it when we drove into town. A big two-story plantation-looking place straight down the road that way." He pointed left. "Do you need to get anything out of your car before you go?"

"Just my luggage," Sam answered.

Jack handed her the keys, and she unlocked the trunk. He helped her by looping one of her faded Vera Bradley bags over the handle of a suitcase and then repeating the process with the other one. "That should make it easy to drag all your stuff up the hill to the B&B. Buster will call you tomorrow, and hopefully, we can meet up for dinner another night."

"We'll see," Sam said curtly. "Thanks for rescuing me again. I hope your meeting goes well."

A vision of the two tumbleweeds popped into her mind as she looped Nibbler's leash around one arm and pulled two suitcases down the cracked sidewalk. "I don't know how I do it, Nibbler, but I draw the wrong ones out of the woodwork anywhere I go," she vented. "Chase Warner was a good churchgoing man—well, I thought so anyway—and see where that got me. Then Jack swoops in like a knight in shining armor and turns out to be a flat-out chronic man-whore. Both have pretty green eyes, and that's my weakness, I know. But I'm stronger than that now." She huffed as she pulled the bag back onto her shoulder and readjusted her carrying arm. "I bet that Jack could talk the underpants off a holy woman—Chase could do that too. They're just a bunch of tumbleweeds. No roots and not an ounce of dependability between the both of them."

CHAPTER TWO

OH, KARA

Not far in Jack's estimation was very different from what that same phrase meant to Sam. She expected a couple or three blocks, but she'd already crossed five streets when she stopped to catch her breath. Standing in front of a closed gift store, she realized that sorry sumbitch was punishing her for not falling for his pickup lines. If she wouldn't go up to his apartment and let him talk her into a bout of sex, then he would make her walk to the B&B.

"Just like a man," she grumbled and started walking again. Her arms were already starting to burn from dragging her suitcases behind her.

In the daylight, Sam supposed the darkened storefronts would be warm and lively, easily inviting tourists into the row of antiques stores, candle shops, and even a leather-working place. But at night with clouds drifting back and forth in front of a mostly full moon, the town square looked like something from one of her shape-shifter romance books. She imagined Jack taking on the shape of a wolf and coming out of one of the alleyways to glare at her with his catlike green eyes.

I will never date another man with eyes like that, she mentally vowed.

The wheels of one of her suitcases hung in a sidewalk crack. The only way she could get it to budge was to unwrap the old Vera Bradley bag from around the handle and sling it over her shoulder. *I've got to start reading more contemporary books, maybe some nonfiction.*

Nibbler tugged at his leash, anxious to get to wherever they were going, the question of dinner probably settling into his mind just like it was in hers. She pulled hard on the suitcase, and the wheels began to move again.

"It can't be much farther, Nibs," she said, more to reassure herself than the dog.

Light filtered out onto the pavement from the window of a building across the street, leaving a long fluorescent streak in the otherwise dark block of closed stores. Iron bars on the windows said that this place didn't want any trouble, but the neon sign flashing OPEN over and over again beckoned customers to come inside for a drink or two, maybe even three.

She crossed over the quiet street and peeked into the window. As soon as she could see inside, she quickly decided that she'd stick out like a sore thumb if she went in with Nibbler and all her baggage. But, still, the thought of a shot of Jack and an ice-cold Coke chaser after a day like this sounded damn good. She hovered for a moment and eyed the door's handle as Nibbler watched her debate internally. Even just a single shot of Maker's or Crown would be good. Fries would be good too; it seemed from Nibbler's facial expressions that he had read her mind and had definitely agreed with her on that particular idea. His tail started to thwack against the metal of the bar door.

She shook her head, forgetting her current mission. First, find this bed-and-breakfast and then a telephone. Those were her next steps, then dinner. Her own phone was currently as useful as a brick. Between car problems, being stranded in a little town, and then having to walk into said little ghost town as it was getting dark, all the key tropes were starting to fall into place to make a run-of-the-mill campy horror movie that in other circumstances, Sam would have secretly loved to have watched. Living the plot of a southern gothic horror—not as much fun as watching it in theaters.

Going to Mena is meant to be a fresh start. Everything is going to be better. Sam kept telling herself that. She was taking full control of her life and determined to write her own storyline from now on. It was time to be her best self—a side mission even to aim for "the clean girl aesthetic"—a term Sam learned at Christmas from her twelve-year-old niece, who knew more about her own skincare than Sam did.

The clean girl aesthetic was described as a mindful woman taking care of herself and investing in herself. *Self-wellness rebranded with new words is still a good thing.* Sam had vowed to implement it in her new life in Mena. Less booze. More yoga. Less burgers and fries. More salads and salmon. To see a child have a more intricate skincare routine than herself had made Sam reel for a bit. She had just turned thirty, which felt like a big thing, but not much had truly changed with the birthday itself. She had started using retinol. She washed her face every night now instead of sleeping in her makeup. That alone was quite a bit of growth already. Hangovers had become gnarlier by the year, so she figured the clean girl method of limiting liquor would have its benefits.

She didn't truly drink that much—unless her heart was broken. There was something about a three-margarita night when a man had let her down that got Sam through the worst of it. There were two dives near Rosepine that Sam knew like the back of her hand from how many times Chase had let her down over the years, and this place seemed to sort of resemble her favorite heartbreak haunt back home. The similarities between this bar and her favorite dive culled when her eyes spotted a small, faded and peeling sign in the corner of the barred window.

NO SHOES, NO SERVICE
NO ANIMALS ALLOWED
NO LOITERING

Saved from bad decisions by the writing on the wall, a rueful little voice whispered in her head in Inez's timbre, and she relayed the bad news down to Nibbler.

"Well, I'm currently loitering and you ain't human. And only one of us has shoes on because the other wouldn't wear our booties that we got at Christmas." Nibbler's ears dropped an inch on cue at this and Sam let out a soft giggle. "Either way, I don't think we add up for their kind of company, so we don't need theirs anyhow."

Nibbler answered with a snort and stomped his front right foot down in the same motion. Sometimes, Sam could swear he understood her every word with the cartoonish way he would make his responses known.

Turning to move, a flicker of blue slid out of the far corner booth and drew Sam's eye back up to the window to see Jack. He was stalking a denim-clad woman on the bar's makeshift dance floor like a panther. She leaned in to get a closer look and recognized the woman as *the* scantily clad Kara she had seen pop up on his phone on the way into town. Once they reached each other, they left no room for Jesus, as Sam's aunt Punkin would've said. They seemed to be completely lost in the way they were clinging to each other. Her denim shorts were cut so short that Sam could see the shadow of Jack's finger flex and squeeze through the white cotton pocket as he cupped her bottom under its frayed hem.

Kara was almost as tall as Jack, her head resting easily on his shoulder. Her other hand raked through his hair as he spun her in lazy circles. Two drunk lovers in their own little world.

"Kara, you have no clue he was trying to get in my pants half an hour ago," she mumbled to the glass.

That boy is a bullet headed for any warm bed he can find, and rest easy, baby, he'll find it. Inez's voice piped in from the back of her mind again.

They seem so happy together. And she doesn't even have a clue that all the while, he's sleeping around. The thought wandered through Sam's mind and awoke something shaky in her, gluing her feet in place.

Did other people know Chase was running around on me before I found out? Was Liza Beth even the only one he ran around on me with, or were there more girls or affairs he just couldn't land. She had found out the hard way that anything was possible with him.

Getting away from the town she grew up in helped her realize she never truly knew the man she loved. Or it turned out, her best friend since childhood either. She had thrown up after driving home and telling her mama, Wanette, about finding them together. Her dad walked in sometime mid-barf, and Wanette caught him up on what had happened. There was something oddly comforting in the way they hovered in the bathroom doorway, unsure how to help but not wanting to leave her alone through the throes of an emotional purging.

"Honey, if he can be taken from you, he can be taken from her. The way you win 'em is the way you lose 'em. He wasn't no good man to begin with, and Liza Beth will see soon enough what she just got into with that Warner boy anyhow. One day that'll be clearer to ya. Uh, I just know that don't probably help much right now." Her dad's voice wandered off as her mother jumped into the conversation.

"Your father's right. I never liked that Liza girl anyway. Her mama was always a snob ever since her husband bought that bank up in Junction City. Such uppity people, we should've known they weren't no good." Wanette started viciously scrubbing around the sink drain with a wet washcloth, keeping her hands busy in a frantic busy-bee manner that she adopted when she was worried. Sam had stared down into the toilet, waiting for the next wave to hit.

She pushed that painful memory to the side and figured that if she stuck around Homestead, she might tell the Kara girl about Jack. Or maybe she'd be smart and just keep her mouth shut. *Let dogs be dogs, and don't get in their way and get bit.*

Her feet unglued themselves from the cement underneath her shoes, and each foot felt ten pounds heavier as she started back walking. "Mama's Broken Heart" filtered out of the bar and followed her across the street and up another block. Sam had watched the video for that song so much she could almost see it playing out in her head as she walked. Good songs helped when the crazy brought on in the aftermath and the reality of everything began rearing its ugly head again.

Her thoughts were becoming as dark as the closed-up stores behind her as she walked on. "I gotta nip this pity party in the bud. If all I do is think about Rosepine, and that dumpster fire of a situation, I haven't left at all and I haven't really accomplished anything." Her voice hitched up on the last word as she hiked her tote back over her shoulder, pausing to get it into a sturdier position before starting to walk again.

"Nibbler, why did you let me pack this much? I didn't need to bring my whole library."

The dog yipped in agreement and kept leading the way.

"It's not far, my ass," she groaned a few minutes later when she looked at the tree-crested hill in front of her and noticed that the sidewalk ended at the end of the block. The floral-patterned straps on her Vera Bradley bag began to slip. She pitched her left shoulder to keep it from hitting the ground, just as her pajama-packed purse fell off her right one.

Nibbler pulled his leash taut, continuing to urge Sam forward, his eyes trained on the flare of lamplight scattered on the sidewalk in front of a single lone shop one block away, the only storefront other than the bar with its lights still on.

Like two little moths in a dark world, they were both pulled to the light source intrinsically. *What a natural thing it is to seek shelter and light when things get dark.* The storefront looked welcoming, even at night.

This feels much less horror movie-ish, Sam's nerves seemed to whisper.

Everbloom Book Shop was scrolled in a lovely looping script in gilded letters across the front window. She scoped the whole front but didn't see any store hours on the window, and not on the door either. But she did see an old black landline phone inside, hung up on a tall cedar column in the middle of the bookshop, seemingly connected to the huge wooden front desk beside it. In the front corner sat two computers side by side on a long antique table with small mismatched leather armchairs in front of each screen. No alarm bells were ringing in her gut so far, and Nibbler seemed keen to go inside, already snuffling loudly at the doorjamb.

She jumped a bit when a bell above her chimed as she eased the door open. *What an incredible place.* Her first thought was simply that. Nibbler yanked Sam forward to inspect this new realm, sniffing everything he could. Hints of recently brewed coffee and old leather surrounded them both, adding to the cozy surroundings. The room was densely packed but tidy, full to its brim with its long rows of books lining every visible patch of wall. *A little library of Alexandria, right here in Texas*, she thought, taking a second to turn in a slow circle and soak it all in.

"Hey, we're closing up!" a man's deep voice yelled from the other side of a beaded curtain that must have led into a back room.

"Oh, yeah! Uh, sorry, I just need some directions," she stammered back, snapping out of the reverie she had fallen in. "Also, I have a small dog. Is it alright if he's in here?"

Heavy footsteps on the hardwood floor told her that someone was headed that way. She waited, expecting to be asked to leave due to Nibbler or closing time.

"You said you need directions? Where are you going this time of day?" The man stood at least six feet tall with thick dark hair that brushed his collar. Broad shoulders and chest, and arms the size of Sam's waist, stretched the knit of his shirt. He took one look at Nibbler and came around the corner of the front desk to drop down on a knee. Big hands, she noticed, that dwarfed Nibbler as he petted the happy dog. "What a cute little puppy. What's his name?"

"Nibbler, and I'm Samantha. I need to double-check if I'm headed in the right direction. I'm looking for the Rose Garden Inn? Or Rose Garden Bed-and-Breakfast? I didn't think it would be this far from the auto shop. Jack said it was only a short walk." She dropped her bags one by one with a thump onto the hardwood floor.

Nibbler rolled over on his back, and the dark-haired man briskly rubbed his stomach.

"Nibbler, you are a very good boy, aren't ya," he said as he straightened up and rounded the counter again and then walked back around with a doggy treat held up in his left hand like a baton.

Nibbler hopped up on his hind feet and did a goofy little dance.

"Okay, okay, that warrants two treats," he said as he went back to grab another from the desk drawer before turning to Sam again. "I'm sorry about that. I was so happy to see a cute little dog, I didn't introduce myself. I'm Noah. To answer your question, it is another quarter of a mile up the hill to the B&B. You take a left out of here and it's straight ahead. Good news is, you don't have much farther in comparison to how far you've already come if you started at the auto shop. Why were you over there?" he asked and then abruptly stuck a hand in his pocket and cut himself off. "You don't have to answer that actually. It's none of my business."

"My car broke down on the highway, and Jack Reynolds took me as far as the garage. I had to leave my car there, so"—she flopped her arms at her sides, pointing to her luggage all spread around on the floor around her feet—"here we are. I had figured it was only a couple of blocks to the B&B when Jack *swore* it wasn't far."

Noah was silent for just a moment before he spoke. "I'll be closing up shop in another half hour. I live on out past Rose Garden, and I'd be happy to take you and Nibbler up there. It's pretty much uphill all the way, and there's no sidewalk after you leave this corner."

Sam thought of Jack and the picture of Kara flashing on his phone. She had lucked out when he didn't turn out to be a serial killer, but maybe she shouldn't tempt fate again by getting in the second strange man's vehicle that she had met today.

She eyed his face. He had warm eyes, a bit hazel, a bit brown, but the lighting wasn't good enough for her to see them fully. But they were warm eyes in any light, wreathed with the new saplings of laugh lines that crinkled even when he smiled just slightly. He had a smattering of freckles across his nose—just a few. She could probably count them.

"Nope," she blurted when she caught herself looking at him too long and took a small step back, "I just needed to make sure that I was on the right path. And to maybe charge my phone and call someone if I wasn't. I'm glad to hear that there actually is a bed-and-breakfast at the end of this wild goose chase." Her voice wandered off, and she looked over her shoulder at the front of the shop. "I saw that you have a couple of computers over there."

"Treats for the dogs, free Wi-Fi for the humans, good for business." Noah's smile quirked higher on one side.

I would love to shoot my folks a message real quick to let them know I'm alright," Sam said. "My cell phone has been dead now for a bit, and I gotta charge it before I can call them."

Noah pointed to the black phone on the column. "Well, you came to the right place. This is a town of limited cell service, but my granddad put in the landline when this place was his. It keeps the lines open in the shop. I have unlimited long-distance. Use that to call them. It's not anything fancy, but it works. I just couldn't get rid of it."

She was used to simply scrolling through recent calls on her phone and pulling her mom's number up, so it took her a minute to punch the number in. If she had been alone, she would've done a jig when it started to ring.

"Hello?" Her mother's tone had a load of concern in it.

"Mama, it's Sam. I'm calling from a bookstore in Homestead, a little town up in northern Texas. My car broke down, but don't worry, I'm safe and I'm about to check into a B&B. I'll stay there until Patsy's fixed."

"I told you," her father called out from somewhere behind her mama. "You wasted your money when you bought that thing. I told you that you should've picked something more dependable."

"I guess you know that you are on speaker phone," her mother said flatly.

"Do we need to come get you and haul the car back down here?" her father asked, his voice louder now, sounding as if he had gotten up out of his armchair and walked closer to where Wanette would be standing in the kitchen.

"No, no, no. I have enough money in my savings to fix whatever it is that's wrong, and I'll be fine," Sam assured them, lying through her teeth. "It seems this place is even smaller than Rosepine. I'm just gonna crash at a B&B not far from this store until I can drive to Greta's. Speaking of, I need to call her next. I'm gonna check into my room, charge my phone, and I'll call y'all tomorrow with more details, okay?"

"Greta was expecting you an hour ago. She called to check in when she hadn't heard from you. She said that she caught an early ride to the airport and was already on the way. That neighbor of hers, Mrs. Myra, I think that's her name, I'm sure she can water the plants and take her mail in 'til you get there. We'll call Greta back now and tell her what all happened. It'll be okay. As long as you're safe, it'll all be fine."

"Don't put any more money in that car!" Her father shouted so loud that Sam yanked the receiver away from her ear with a wince.

"I love y'all. I got this handled, I promise." Sam said her farewells and put the receiver back on its base. She turned to find Noah sitting cross-legged on the floor with Nibbler in his lap. "Thanks for letting me use your phone, and for the directions as well."

"No problem at all." Noah stood up with Nibbler draped over his arms like a limp rag. Sam sympathized with the little dog. With his short legs doing double time on the long walk from the auto shop, Nibbler had to be worn out. And after the emotional upheaval of the day, *she* was as mentally exhausted as her poor dog was physically.

"Alright, little one, we gotta hit the road and find you some dinner." She rubbed the ear of the sleepy-eyed mutt, still splayed back into Noah's right arm.

Noah picked up one of her bags from the floor with his free hand and draped it over her shoulder. When his fingertips slipped just a touch and brushed her bare neck, a wildfire traveled down her spine.

No, no! Absolutely not! Jack said that he has a girlfriend, Sam scolded herself. *Off-limits, off-limits, off-limits, this is all off-limits!* The sirens screamed and flashed in her mind, snapping her back a bit as he leaned closer to help load the second bag onto her other shoulder.

"Wait a minute. I got a better idea." Noah stopped and turned to slip the bag onto the bigger suitcase's handles, with Nibbler supervising from his roost in Noah's other arm.

He moved around easily, homed in on the problem, solving her luggage ordeal as she just stood there, internally electrocuted.

Your body shouldn't have reacted that way, her brain chided in a shrill, tinny voice.

This man could never know that his touch affected her like that. The flush that pricked her cheeks snapped her back to what he was doing.

"I did that too, and it worked 'til I hit a crack in the sidewalk." Her voice sounded high-pitched in her own ears.

He stopped layering the duffel bags, took a step back, and looked at the bags as if calculating something. "Are you sure I can't give you a ride or at least walk you up to Ms. Kathleen's?" he finally asked.

"No, really, I can do it myself. Thank you again though for everything. You said your name was Noah, right?" she answered.

"Good memory. And anytime," Noah said with a genuine smile. He set Nibbler on the floor, picked up a flashlight from the counter behind him, and held it out to her. "Take this."

With a suitcase handle in each hand, Nibbler's leash tied around her left wrist, and her purse over her other shoulder, she looked purposefully from one of her hands to the other and looked back up at him.

"I'd need a third hand," she said.

Noah set the flashlight back down on the counter, picked up a dark blue necktie from his desk and tied the two suitcases together within a matter of seconds. "Now, you have a land train if you insist on walking. Are you one hundred percent sure I can't give you a ride?"

"Nibbler and I can make it, but thanks again."

He looked like he was going to say something more but instead turned to grab the flashlight again. She took it this time when he offered it to her. She held it up as if weighing the heavy thing.

"Is this for protection or what?"

Noah walked her to the door and held it open for her. "There's nothing but woods growing between my store and Ms. Kathleen's. It will give you some light. I guess it could serve as a club if any vicious raccoon or bloodthirsty possum thinks you and Nibbler here look like a treat. But that's all you have to fear in those woods," he said with a smile. "In all honesty, it just gets a bit spooky going up that hill in the dark by yourself sometimes."

"It's probably all those bloodthirsty possums."

He smiled a bit wider and walked outside of the shop with her, letting the door chime and close behind him.

"You're probably right, it's most likely the possums."

Sam got a whiff of something pleasant that was separate from the homey smell in the shop—old books, yes, but also a bit of sawdust, and a little worn leather and aftershave.

He has a girlfriend, walk away right now if you got one lick of shame in you.

Sam wished Inez was wrong, but that little voice from her old friend that normally sounded in her gut had always led her in the right direction, and she knew to listen.

"I'll return your tie and this weapon of mass destruction"—she held up the hefty flashlight again—"before I leave."

"I ain't worried about that. I got too many ties anyhow. Same goes for flashlights. I keep 'em in every nook and corner of the shop—if the wind finds a way to blow through the trees, or if a mockingbird sings too loud in a nearby town, the electricity goes out. I try to stay prepared." His warm eyes crinkled at the corners, and like an old map folding easily into the faint lines left from past creases, the small lines around his eyes deepened.

"Maybe I'll see you around if you get bored and burn through the little library you got stashed. I can sense a bookworm when I meet one." He nodded to the biggest duffel bag she carried, over-filled with her books, their pointy edges poking Sam in her ribs with each step.

She laughed a bit at this. "Well, if Buster can't find the parts quick, I'll come visit. I guess I won't have anything better to do but read 'til I'm back on the road."

He leaned back against the doorjamb. "I'm here from nine to seven most every day except Sundays. Since today is Valentine's, a late order rush has me working longer than normal. But hey, turns out someone needed directions, and fate had it that I was here to help them."

Sam hated that for a moment, and she wondered what his supposed girlfriend thought of him working late on Valentine's Day.

"Well." She cleared her throat and nodded to Noah. "Thanks again."

He waved her off, and his hand settled back on the doorknob. "Anytime!" He was still smiling when she turned and started off in the direction of twinkling warm lights sprinkling through the dense pines like little stars beaming through the night sky.

Hopefully, that was the B&B up ahead. When Noah had pointed that way, her eyes had followed past his finger to a little windy gravel drive into the tree line. She only made it about twenty steps off the sidewalk's end before she had to flick on the flashlight to keep from stepping into a second muddy pothole like she just had the first one, not ten seconds before.

He was right, she mused as she swung the heaviest suitcase over the next rough patch in the path with a grunt. *The flashlight was a good idea.*

One man cheated on her.

Another sent her out in the dark.

The third gave her light and his necktie.

"Let's guess which one just might be trustworthy," she muttered.

Sam stopped several times to catch her breath as she walked up the hill, the whole while her thoughts flip-flopping between green-eyed men and the blister on the back of her left heel, the ache beginning to push itself to the front burner of her mind now. How the hell did she find herself dragging overpacked suitcases up a gravel drive in the middle of the night in the middle of a nowhere town?

She was puffing out short breaths by the time she reached the lane that led up to the looming two-story house, and she realized it was the same place that she had spotted earlier on the drive into town with Jack. The memory of watching *Gone with the Wind* with her memaw when she was eleven came to her mind, specifically the moment when the camera centered on Tara, Scarlett's family home, for the first time. Her eyes widened now in the same way they did back then when Tara came into view on the little twelve-inch TV on her memaw's kitchen counter.

A pickup honked as it passed behind her on the main road, and Sam turned as Noah stuck his hand out the window and waved, driving on to what Sam supposed was his house farther up the way. She waved back and trudged the last few steps to the white wrought iron fence that surrounded the front of the place. Sam pushed the gate open with the side of her smaller suitcase and shuffled into the front yard, dragging her baggage caravan over the cobblestone walkway, the wheels clunking out a staccato melody as Nibbler continued to lead the way.

With light from the moon and half a dozen fancy brass lanterns hanging every five or six feet from the gate to the house, she could easily see her way now. Bounded on both sides of the walkway in thick brambles were the reddest roses Sam had ever seen, all in different stages of blooming, some starting to bud, others heavy with blooms. They shone a brilliant bloodred under the brass light fixtures, and honestly, they almost looked fake.

Sam wondered just how many more bushes there had to be around the property to make it smell so strongly of roses. The walkway was well lit, but on past what she could see in the flashlight's beam, darkness loomed for what seemed like forever before meeting the trees again at the back end of the property. Clouds shifted back and forth over the moon, offering soft shapes in the distance. She turned off the flashlight and slipped it under her arm as she breathed in the scent that clung on the brisk night air. Roses and white pine, she guessed, maybe something else underneath, but the closer she got to the house, the thicker the scent of roses became. The fine trace of pine sap underlined the heady floral smell and slipped like a ribbon from the top of the aroma as the pines fell farther into the background.

"No wonder this place is called the Rose Garden," she whispered as she walked up the front steps and reached up to grab the heavy brass knocker. Before she could even touch the lion's head, the door flew open. Sam had imagined a tall, angular, gaunt older gentleman in long tails would answer a door like this—a butler trained to look down his nose at guests for showing up outside of visiting hours, demanding a calling card in some bored drawl.

But an old woman of short stature jerked Sam back to the present when she swung the big door open instead.

"I'm Kathleen Scott, and I've been expecting you," she said as she adjusted a strap of her bibbed overalls.

Stumped and shocked, Sam blurted out, "How?"

"Come in." The lady ignored the question and motioned her inside with a flick of her wrist. "Samantha, is it? Noah called and said you were on the way. Small Texas towns thrive on gossip, honey. Buster told his wife, Allie, about you and your dog when he got home. She made a couple of calls, and soon all the phone lines were on fire about a redheaded woman whose hot rod gave out on the highway and is stuck here in Homestead now. Then Noah called. So, I'd guessed you'd be here soon enough. I have a room all ready for you."

"Wow! I knew word traveled fast in a small town, and I guess for once I'm glad it did. Thank you for getting a room ready for me." She went back down the steps to start pulling her things into the house. "Most folks call me Sam, this is Nibbler."

"Oh, just look at this sweet little baby." She bent down with a nimbleness that surprised Sam and started scratching Nibbler's neck around his collar. His tail picked up speed when her nails found the sweet spot near his sternum.

"My precious Waylon died two years ago. He was just a few months old when I found him, all ate up with ticks in a ditch out near the McClemmins' farm. He was just a purebred mutt if I ever saw one, but in all my years, he was the best dog I've ever had. He's buried in the backyard. You'll have to see his tombstone while you are here. It's shaped like a soup bone. I imagine half the toys and bones I bought for him are buried all over the yard. You can have a little scavenger hunt while you're here, Mr. Nibbler."

"I can't imagine what it looks like during the day out here. I could smell the roses before the house even came into view. I was surprised to see them blooming this early," Sam said.

"I've worked with them for more than forty years to make them hearty enough to leaf out and set some buds by Valentine's Day. We clip the good ones each year—they are a specialty at the flower shop," Kathleen said.

"She grows them, and I sell 'em." A lady even shorter than Kathleen appeared from a room to the right. "I'm Loretta, and while Kathleen piddles around with her roses and runs this place, I make the arrangements and take care of the flower shop in the old carriage house."

"And she lives here now that she's got so old she can't climb the stairs in her old garage apartment," Kathleen added plainly.

Loretta shook her finger at Kathleen. "Be careful calling me old, Katty. You're just as old as me." The little woman turned back to look up at Sam. "Our front room girl had to quit today. Are you interested in a little job while you are here? I've put out the word that I need some help, but only Brenda Lewis has applied."

From the look Loretta shot Kathleen at the mentioning of Brenda and the extra flair Loretta put on the lady's name, Sam guessed that Brenda was a no-go as a candidate for whatever this job was.

"Oh, no, you don't!" Kathleen stood up straighter and stared at Loretta. "You will not poach her from me! I was going to see if she'd fill in for Vivian until her car was fixed."

"Fill in for what? What's a front room girl?" Sam asked, looking from one woman's stubborn expression to the next. She had walked through the front door no more than a minute before, and already she had been slung midway into a sales pitch for two new jobs from a couple of old women bickering back and forth in the expansive wainscoted hallway. She hadn't even gotten a room or put her luggage down just yet. And she needed to pee and eat and get some sleep so her brain would function right.

"It's easy work. I need someone to run the register, take orders when customers call in, talk to everybody when they come in," Loretta explained. "We've got two funerals and a wedding on the books for this coming week. I'll be spending most of my time making floral arrangements. All I'm saying is, I need more hands on deck than Kathleen does right now."

They were as different as night and day in their looks. Loretta was snack-sized, couldn't have weighed more than a hundred pounds if she was soaking wet and had rocks in the pockets of her cobalt blue velour jogging suit. Little frame, big hair. Sam figured that she could hide a kitten in Loretta's 1960s-style bouffant.

A bound of gray hair that had been teased and sleeked tidily into shape gave her a few inches more height than Kathleen, and there was not a hair out of place, Sam noted. Loretta reminded Sam a little of her memaw. The faint smell of Elnett hair spray that wafted around the little woman took Sam back to her childhood, spraying the sticky starchy mess on her own hair when her memaw was in another room. It smelled like childhood spent with her grandparents compressed into a can.

Kathleen might have been two inches taller than Loretta sans her bouffant, but neither woman reached Sam's shoulder.

Kathleen's faded overalls had a patch on one knee and a tear on the other, her white T-shirt smeared with the day's dirt. Her salt-and-pepper hair, heavy on the salt, was scraped back and twisted into a French roll. A few strands had escaped, and she had tucked them behind her ears.

Sam felt instantly at home here. Maybe it was because Kathleen reminded her of Inez Walters, her elderly friend from church, the wise old sage, as Sam jokingly referred to her friend before she had passed. Inez always had Skittles in her purse to sneak Sam during the service when she was younger, and she invited her and her parents to Sunday dinner often as Sam grew up.

You can trust these women. They are good people. Inez's voice was so clear that Sam scanned the room to see if she was really there.

"Why can't I do both, like the other woman did?" Sam asked.

"Do you know how to set a table or cook breakfast?" Kathleen asked.

Before Sam could even answer, Loretta hopped in, "How about running a cash register?"

"I guess I can do both, but I literally just met you two. I'm sorry, I just don't get why y'all are both offering me a job. Why did the other woman leave?"

"She gave her notice three weeks ago because she is expecting her first and didn't plan to work after the baby was born," Loretta said. "But she went into labor early and delivered a sweet little girl last night. I thank the Lord that baby held off until after Valentine's Day. And that it's healthy, of course," Loretta plopped in at the end.

"And we trust Noah," Kathleen added.

"What has he got to do with anything?" Sam asked.

"He's a good man, and he says that you are good people," Loretta answered.

"I was only in his store a few minutes," Sam argued.

"He's not a wizard or anything, but he's pretty good at reading people. He's honed that over the years. He said that you called your parents and talked kindly to them, and that anyone who loves a dog like you do has to be a fine human being," Kathleen replied with a little smirk. "And if he's wrong for the first time, I can just kick you out the same door you came in."

"You'll get room and board too. It's minimum wage but it ain't hard work and payroll goes out each week on Fridays." The little lady wiggled her drawn-on eyebrows as she drew out the word *Friday*, pronouncing it "Fry-Dee." "And of course, if you leave before then, we'll tally up your hours."

The whole scene was uncanny and more than a little surreal. She asked herself the question she had been asking all day. How did she end up here? Did God plan all these little kinks in her journey to lead her here? Hadn't she asked him for a new start and a good distraction? Is that what this was?

She thought of how Buster's tone changed once he looked under the hood earlier today. She could make money while she waited, help these ladies out, get free room and board and save there too. She weighed her options and bit her lip. Or she could drain her bank account on Patsy, wait around doing nothing, and just pray she had enough money to cover all the parts and labor. *God shuts doors and opens windows*, she thought as she took a deep breath and let it out slowly. Sometimes climbing through the window is the best option when the house is on fire.

She took one more breath and finally nodded. "I don't know how long I'm gonna be here, but Buster down at the auto shop said it could be several days before he found all the parts to fix my car.

So, I will gladly take the job." She added after a pause at the end, "You know, for now."

She could have squeezed Noah for giving her such a glowing recommendation, but then she remembered the sparks. Maybe she'd just write him a thank-you card or buy some books from him while she was there.

"Have you had supper yet?" Kathleen asked. "We were about to sit down to some tomato soup and grilled cheese on my town-renowned sourdough bread."

"We haven't had anything since around noon. That sounds delicious," Sam answered.

"I've got dog food left over from when my Waylon was still with me, so we'll feed the pup too. We'll get Nibbler some nibbles." Kathleen seemed pleased with her play on words. "After we finish dinner, we'll put your things on the lift and send y'all up to the second floor."

"The lift?" I asked.

"The dumbwaiter," Loretta interjected. "In the back of the kitchen. Kathleen's folks had it put in when they built this place over a hundred years ago."

"My great-grandmother entertained a lot back in the days when this place was first built," Kathleen explained. "The hired help used it to take things up and down. Laundry, room service, and that kind of thing."

"It's handier each year since Kathleen's just getting older and older." Loretta sighed theatrically.

Kathleen narrowed her eyes into slits. "Enough of that."

"You know I love you more than I do sex," Loretta teased.

"You ain't got any of that in so long, I'm surprised you still remember what that word means." Kathleen laughed and Loretta cackled as they both went about setting the table for Sam to join them.

"Besides, back when you were younger, knowing you and your prowess round town—well I can bet my left foot you might've said that to me, but there was no way it could've been the truth. I remember the younger wilder Loretta." Kathleen had a light sparking deep in her eyes as if a certain funny memory had come to mind.

"Oh, I remember her too," Loretta responded with wry smile.

"I think we'd both need to buy a how-to book to even know how to go about that stuff these days."

"Hey now, Katty, speak for yourself!" Loretta scolded and folded a paper towel in half and slid it under Sam's dish.

Sam hopped in and offered, "The old saying is it's like riding a bicycle: once you know how, you never forget it."

Kathleen let out a full throaty laugh at this, holding one plate in her hand as she turned to the women and shrugged. "One thing I never learned how to do was ride a bike."

"Aw, well, that's sad, Kathleen. Bikes are fun, maybe you should hop back on one and give it a try some time," Loretta said, wiggling her painted-on eyebrows again before winking. All three women broke into laughter, and the dining room chandelier seemed to shiver from the uproar of the women.

Oh, yes, ma'am, Sam was going to love it at the Rose Garden.

CHAPTER THREE

HOW LONG

The Rose Garden had a very different vibe the week after Valentine's Day. It'd been quiet as a graveyard the night Sam got there, but by Sunday night, all nine of the extra bedrooms were filled. The ancient house came alive again with the sound of jovial arguing and laughter coming from the library on the first floor and the smell of coffee in the kitchen rising to meet the conversation chatter, beckoning sleepy travelers to come down for breakfast. Sam was told to remind the guests that tea, coffee, snacks, and waters were available all day and evening on the buffet in the dining room.

Several of the customers that she helped at breakfast also sought out the same electric tea kettle that she set out in the evening, and they chatted as the kettle warmed. The guests were normally very kind and predictably a tad charmed by the house, as Sam still was. Like clockwork, every guest's first words were always something about the gardens. There was something almost militant in the caliber Kathleen kept the gardens to, and the hours she kept tending the garden. And it showed.

The house was a tiny, ever-changing city within itself. It seemed to pull in all kinds as far as clientele, from green thumbs to an occasional bird watcher or oil riggers with the weekend off, stopping over on their way to the next site. No matter who was staying, the chamomile seemed to be the slot in the wooden tea box on the buffet that Sam noticed would routinely be empty by eight p.m. Sam was constantly going to the kitchen to fetch some bags for the other tea-seeking night owls.

For the most part, Kathleen would help Sam whip up breakfast, and after it was served, leave the visitors to entertain themselves if the weather permitted. She'd soon retreat into her jungle of roses to prune and tend once again. Sam found the routine easy to fall into and caught on quickly. Her favorite part of the day was getting to visit with the guests over breakfast. She'd soak up as many stories as she could in the mornings before heading across the massive yard to the old carriage house with Nibbler in tow to help Loretta at the flower shop.

Loretta loved old country music—Waylon, Willie, Johnny Cash, Patsy Cline, Loretta Lynn, and all those folks—and kept it going in the shop from opening to closing. That era was what Sam had cut her teeth on, and she never got tired of listening to it. Her mornings started with coffee, bacon, and people happy to chat, and her afternoons were a swirl of Hank, Haggard, and the smell of flowers. By the time half of the week had passed by, she had an odd sense of settled.

That morning, Loretta had gone to deliver a couple of arrangements, and Sam was alone in the shop when the store's landline rang. She grabbed the receiver from the wall and said, "Rose Petal Flower Shop. This is Samantha."

"I'm glad you answered," a vaguely familiar voice said. "This is Buster from down at Jack's Auto, and I've got some bad news.

The deeper I get into your car's problems, the more I'm finding. It looks like it's gonna cost a pretty penny to set Patsy right. It also may take me a good bit of time to locate the parts, then line up the labor to get y'all back on the road safely."

"How long and how much you thinking?" Sam crossed her fingers on her other hand.

"A real rough estimate is seven thousand dollars, and that's hoping that I can find what I need and the shipping's cheap. Since Mr. Miller retired last summer and closed his shop, I'm the only mechanic in this area, so it'd have to be a side project here in the shop. It will take at least a month or longer for me to even start on it. And like I said, that's if I can locate parts. I can get some of them new, but they'll be pricier." He sighed. "My advice is to sell it for the body and let someone else take care of the restoration."

Sam was glad the phone had a long cord attached to it because she slid down to the floor and propped her back against the wall. She didn't even have half that in her savings account, and it would take months and months to earn the rest with her job at the B&B and flower shop.

"Can I have some time to think about it?" she finally asked.

"Sure, take all the time you need. I'll make a list of all the parts and then wait for you to let me know what you want done. I can park it around back in our junk lot until you decide," Buster said. "I'm sorry I don't have better news. I'd buy the body myself and fix it up, but my wife would kill me. I have connections with some guys with lots of money who love old models and would jump at a chance to get their hands on a body in this good of shape." Buster had a hopeful note in his voice for a second but when she didn't answer, he asked, "I noticed your vanity plate says Patsy. Is she named for Patsy Cline?"

"Yes, she is." Sam could barely answer around the lump in her throat.

"My wife and I two-stepped together to 'Crazy' on our first date down at Scottie's," Buster said. "That was ten years ago now. Time flies, I swear. I'll wait for your call on Patsy, alright?"

"Yes, and thank you." Sam reached up, put the receiver back on the base and buried her head in her hands. As if on cue, "Crazy" was the next song on Loretta's playlist, and "I Fall to Pieces" followed right behind it.

Loretta came in through the back door and tossed her purse on the worktable before she eased down on the floor beside Sam. "Good Lord, girl, what has happened? Did someone die?"

"Patsy is on her deathbed," Sam sobbed. "It's terminal, and I can't save her."

Loretta sucked in a little breath and leaned closer to wrap her arms around Sam's shoulders. "Who is Patsy, and is it cancer?"

"She's not a person. She's my 1965 Mustang, and according to Buster, she has complete organ failure." Sam wept even harder.

"I have trusted Buster with my vehicles for years. If he says she's on life support, then you should pull the plug and let her go. Why did you name her Patsy?" Loretta asked.

"My sorry-ass boyfriend cheated on me, and Patsy's songs helped me get through. Before that, she didn't have a name," Sam explained between hiccups.

"Well, darlin', when you get ready to say goodbye to her, Kathleen and I will go with you," Loretta said.

The bell above the front door rang.

"I'll get it this time. You go wash your face and put on a smile. You ain't alone in this. It'll be okay," Loretta promised and popped up on her feet like a teenager.

* * *

A week passed before Samantha was ready to "pull the plug" as Loretta had called it. On Friday night, Sam called her mother and asked her not to put it on speaker.

"Your father is at the church for a men's supper," she said. "What's going on?"

Sam broke down and sobbed out the story of the car, ending with, "I'm going to sell her tomorrow to a guy who restores and keeps vintage cars in a museum somewhere in New Mexico. I don't wanna tell Daddy yet. Not today. The guy is coming to get her tomorrow, so this evening Kathleen, Loretta, and I are going by the shop to tell her goodbye."

"I'm sorry, Sam," Wanette said. "I know how much that car meant to you, but honey, all things die eventually, past loves fade away, good cars stop cranking. You are doing the right thing. Patsy will be taken good care of. It's like she'll be going to car heaven and reincarnated in a new life."

For her Southern Baptist mother to bring up reincarnation, Sam knew she was trying her best to soothe her daughter from hundreds of miles away. "Thank you for listening, Mama," Sam said and pulled a few more squares off the roll of Angel Soft that she had squirreled to her room from the bathroom. She had folded and refolded one soggy square so much it had ripped as her mother kept talking.

"Can we drive up there now and bring you home?"

"No, I think I'm going to stay for a while longer, Mama. I'm sad about Patsy. I'm wrecked, really. But I like it here. I'm kinda shocked how easily I have meshed into a good routine. It can be pretty busy sometimes, but I've enjoyed it. The irony of escaping Rosepine to a place called Rose Garden doesn't escape me, but Greta said that Mrs. Myra was willing to tend to everything 'til she gets back. I checked with her the other day, and I kinda love the two jobs I have, and Nibbler likes it here too." Sam was rambling and stopped herself.

"Well, when you get ready to come home, just give us a call, and Sam . . ." Wanette paused. "I think you may be transferring all the grief you have about Chase and Liza Beth to your car. Liza Beth was your best friend for twenty-five years, honey. Losing someone in this way will wreck you as badly as if they had truly died. You are experiencing all the stages of grief. I just hope you find some peace up there in that little town."

"Me too, Mama." Sam sighed. "I'll call again soon unless a cricket farts. We never know when we'll lose reception up here on the hill. Between the landline at the bookshop and the B&B though, you can reach me if there's an emergency. I'll let you know how the funeral goes."

Loretta rapped on the doorframe and poked her head inside Sam's room. "Sorry, I didn't know you were on the phone. Kathleen and I are ready when you are. No rush."

"Bye, Mama. I love you." Sam ended the call and nodded toward Loretta. "I'm ready."

Kathleen drove her Cadillac to the auto shop so slowly that Sam felt like they were really in a funeral procession. Loretta sat in the front seat in a flowing black skirt topped off with a black-and-white-striped sweater. Kathleen's customary overalls had been replaced with a black pantsuit, marking what a special occasion it was.

Sam hadn't realized till then, but she had never seen Kathleen in anything but her overalls since landing in Homestead. Sam had chosen her nicest pair of wide-leg jeans and pulled on a Patsy Cline T-shirt she had bought on a girls' trip to Nashville that she and Liza Beth took shortly after buying her car. She hated the memories that bombarded her when she had pulled it from her suitcase, but it seemed like the right shirt to wear to say goodbye.

When they arrived, Buster escorted them through the auto shop and into the junkyard out back. Patsy looked like she would run just fine if Sam got into the front seat and started the engine, but that was not going to happen. The car had been with her through thick and thin, from apartment to apartment in college, from dive bars to road trips, and now it lay dead in a car cemetery in the little town it led her to. Her last job seemed to be the mission of bringing Sam to Homestead to heal her broken heart.

Sam opened the passenger door and removed all the personal items from the glove compartment, then closed it again. She braced herself against the idea of walking away from her beloved car, but she couldn't control the tears flooding her cheeks.

"You know all my secrets and listened to me cry too many times to count," she said as she laid her hand on the hood. "I will miss you so much, but you're going to a better place."

She felt Noah's presence long before turning to find him standing a few feet behind her. "I'm so sorry for your loss," he said as he handed her one of the four red roses he had brought.

"Thank you. What are you doing here?" Sam said as she laid the rose on the hood of the car.

Kathleen and Loretta followed suit with Noah placing the last rose on Patsy's hood beside the others before stepping closer to Samantha. "Kathleen told me you were having a funeral today. Giving up anything that you love is like going through a death. If you need a quiet place to grieve or distract yourself from this, there's a nook in the back corner of the bookshop with a couple of comfy chairs. Reading is a good escape from the harsh realities of the world."

"I appreciate that, and I might take you up on the offer," she said.

"It's the least a friend can do," he replied with a soft smile.

Kathleen draped an arm around Sam's shoulders. "Maybe you can swing by the bookstore tomorrow evening after the flower shop closes. I need to return a couple books and get some more for next week, so I'd appreciate it if you would run that errand for me."

"I can do that." Sam sniffled.

Noah pulled a stark white handkerchief from his pocket and handed it to Sam. "I gotta head back to the store. I'll see you tomorrow, then."

Who carries around an actual handkerchief these days? Sam wondered as she took the folded napkin from Noah. One day, she vowed, she'd ask him about his childhood.

"Thank you," she said and dabbed at her wet cheeks with the soft hanky. She took one last look at Patsy and finally walked back into the shop.

Jack came out of the office as they entered and flashed a brilliant smile Sam's way—one that still reminded Sam of a wolf—yes, sir, wolfish was the perfect description for Jack.

"Samantha, it's good to see you again. Buster tells me that you are selling that Mustang. If you need a ride anywhere or just get lonely and want some company, I'm your guy, darlin'. I'll be glad to take you wherever you want to go," he said in a low, seductive voice.

Kathleen seemed to bristle at that, suddenly looped her arm into Sam's, and turned their backs to Jack to walk to the exit. Her voice was two notches above a cat's hiss as she said, "If she needs anything or anyone, Loretta and I will take care of her."

Sam looked back to holler goodbye to Buster, and then the gaggle of women walked out of the open garage door, making their way to Kathleen's Cadillac in silence.

"You be careful of Jack. He's broken a lot of hearts here in Homestead, and I don't reckon he's finished with the job yet. If there's a wolf in sheep's clothing in this town's flock, it's him," Loretta whispered when they were back in Kathleen's car.

"I'm thinking the same thing," Sam told her.

On Saturday evening, Kathleen ushered Sam and Nibbler out the door with a tote bag full of books. "Poor little critter loves the big backyard, but a break from his patrol duties would do him good. It's hard work putting the fear of God into every critter in Homestead. Now, Nibbler"—Kathleen bent down and cupped his face in her hands—"if a bear comes out of the woods, you drag Sam back here as fast as you can. Do you understand me?"

He yipped as if he actually understood and licked her hand.

"Good boy, now get along and don't stay out too late," Kathleen said, waving them off from the front porch before going back inside.

Going down the hill in the daylight was a lot different from climbing it in the dark. Nibbler pranced down the lane, testing the length of the leash, pulling Sam along. "Hold on, boy. I'm sure there's not enough dogs in this place to have wiped out all the treats at the bookstore. You don't have to hurry. Stop and smell the roses."

The smell of pine sap and fresh rosebuds swirled around Sam as they walked down the drive. She sniffed the air just as Nibbler did. "I bet everyone knows when the roses start blooming. The scent probably stretches out from here to Jefferson when the garden's in full bloom."

Maybe God brought her here on purpose. The longer she was in this little town, the more firmly she just knew there was a reason fate had brought her there. Something in her gut told her so, though she couldn't identify what it was quite yet. Being as hardheaded as her mama, sometimes it took God slapping her upside the head to steer Sam into the right direction.

The biggest plot twist Sam had experienced since the nauseating scandal of finding Chase and Liza Beth sleeping together was Patsy breaking down and leaving her in Homestead to nurse her heart back to health. She now had two new wise sages, a term she used dotingly for Inez and now Loretta and Kathleen had earned as well. She had a friend in town her age too—the local bookworm Noah. Buster had helped sell Patsy for a decent price, and with the money now in her savings, he was helping her look for a newer model of the old Mustang of days past. Two jobs and an airy room with three giant windows were ready for Sam to just step into and start over. Inez had been right when she told her that there was joy on the other side of pain.

She found herself humming the melody of "Believe" by Cher all the way down the hill. She was only a few yards from the sidewalk when Jack stopped his pickup right beside her and stuck his head out the window. "Hello, gorgeous, do you need a ride?"

"No, thank you," she said, forcing herself to not roll her eyes as she kept walking.

"We could have some good times if you'd loosen up a little," he said sourly.

She stopped and glared at him. "I'm sure there are plenty of women who are loose enough for you in this town already."

"Jealous, are we?" He drove along beside her at a creeping pace, and she didn't answer. "You can't take that dog into any of the stores or leave him tied outside either. Someone will call animal control, and they'll take him to the pound."

She stopped in front of the bookstore and smiled sweetly at Jack with her best "eat shit" grin. "Not this one. Goodbye, Jack."

"Hit the Road Jack" came to her mind and made her grin as she opened the door.

"You'll change your mind about me eventually," he called out.

"When pigs fly and hell freezes over," she shot back at him and closed the door in his face.

Noah poked his head up over a pile of books on a nearby table, his eyes warming with a welcoming smile. "Well, hello, Samantha. I thought I might see you today."

"Hello to you too. I'm returning some books. I'm not sure how you and Kathleen do this, but here's what I'm supposed to give to you," Sam said.

Noah got to his feet, went to the desk, and took two treats from the drawer. "Hello to you too, Nibbler. Did that walk down here wear you out?"

The dog flopped down onto the floor and let out a haggard harrumph.

"If you hadn't realized yet, he's the king of drama," Sam said with a giggle.

Noah slid a wink toward her. "Not Nibbler! He's a perfect boy. He just needs something to sustain him so he can make the trip back up to the B&B." He tossed the two treats up in the air, and the dog caught both in his mouth.

"Now that the important business is over, let's talk books. What is Kathleen interested in this week?"

"She said for me to pick something out, but I could use some help," Sam answered. "Does she run a tab or . . ."

"She and Loretta have a special deal here. Kathleen and I did our best to get a library started here in Homestead, but it didn't happen. We'll keep trying until we succeed, but until then, I let her and Loretta use the store as a library. They read the books, return them, and I put them back on the shelves. Everything in here is used anyway, so it doesn't hurt them to get read one more time."

"How do you ever make a living that way?" Sam asked.

"I do most of my business online and by mailing the orders out," Noah answered. "So, what do my two best readers want this week?"

She scanned the store and saw piles of books on the tables, a long stretch behind the counter with cubbyholes stuffed full of rolled up maps and documents, and walls covered with marked shelves: mystery, romance, sci-fi, historical, paranormal and nonfiction. "I'm not sure. I'm returning two cowboy romances from Loretta and a couple of historical romances and autobiographies that Kathleen just finished. Can I just prowl around for a while?"

"As much as you want, and like I told you yesterday, there's a nice little reading cove behind the beaded curtain, and there's coffee and snacks," he answered. "I'm gonna get to work cataloging that bunch over on the table that came in this week. I've got some readers who are interested in the older Mary Stewart novels, especially first editions of *The Moon-Spinners*."

"Didn't she pass away recently?" Sam asked as she chose a historical romance book from the shelf and headed toward the back room.

"No, but her backstock will be harder to find as time goes by," Noah replied.

It smelled like a new pot of coffee had been brewed recently, so Sam pulled a beige mug from the sideboard and filled her cup before pouring herself into one of the overstuffed leather chairs in the back nook. Nibbler jumped up on the sister chair beside her and turned around a couple of times before collapsing on the cushion and promptly falling asleep.

"That little jaunt down the hill really did wear you out, didn't it?" Sam whispered to the normally energetic dog, and she opened her book. She read five pages before she realized that she couldn't even remember the hero's name. She saw the words, but they weren't registering.

Her thoughts were on a fast-moving merry-go-round with the gear shift stuck in reverse—her first date with Chase rising up in her mind. They had gone to a nice Italian restaurant, he had pulled her chair out, bought her dinner, and walked her to her door later that night. All the makings of a true gentleman.

Her first call once his taillights faded from her driveway was to Liza Beth. She went on and on about him to Liza, as a girl does with her best friend after a hopeful first date.

Her mind skipped over the past like a stone on smooth water to another memory. She and Liza Beth peering over smudgy glass cases, oohing and aahing, arguing over the cut of diamonds, and pointing at the rings they wanted one day.

"Go uptown and figure out what you like, Sam, I wanna get you a ring you like," Chase had said one night while they lay in bed, watching the ceiling fan circle, as their breath slowed after a bout of lovemaking. They talked about children and houses and ring sizes. And somewhere in between all their newfound plans and the fodder surrounding them, the little voice in Sam's gut that screamed that Chase was running around on her was successfully stamped out by all the hope Chase poured into her heart.

She was raised on happily ever afters. From Disney movies to Harlequin romances, she didn't watch or read anything unless it had a nice ending. And maybe, just maybe, she would have one too if she played her cards right. He wasn't perfect, but Liza reminded her often that no man was. She picked out a ring she liked at the jewelry shop, just as Liza did—for shits and giggles even though Liza was single at the time—and went back with Chase later to show him the one she liked. She guessed he would plan to propose closer to Christmas because it was her favorite holiday, or maybe her birthday that summer.

But it didn't happen that year or the next—or for her birthday, or Valentine's Day, or any other time.

Chase said that he loved her. Liza had repeatedly reminded her that she was crazy to doubt him, but the little inner voice got louder and louder the longer that he spoke of marriage but didn't propose. That itching suspicion that something had changed in the last few months had followed her like a shadow into every conversation they had. He was still attentive for the most part but distracted in a new way. He wasn't the knight in shining armor anymore. Just a man who always had to work late. Who kept his phone face down and on silent at all times. Sam had painted him to be like the hero and love interest in one of her books. But he wasn't. He never was. He was just a man.

Sam opened the book to the first page to start all over again. Chase had ruined a lot of things in her life, but she refused to let his memory step foot into Homestead. She took a breath and started back at chapter one.

She didn't hear the door chime, but Nibbler must have. He woke up and growled down deep in his throat, then jumped down off the chair and became a furry blur as he ran past her. He was on his way out the open door with Sam following after him when Noah caught him by the collar and picked him up. Still growling, he tried to wiggle free of his arms.

"I'm so sorry if he ran off a customer. He doesn't normally act like that with people, only squirrels and cats," she apologized a little breathlessly.

"Well, evidently, he doesn't like Jack Reynolds," Noah chuckled, "but there's no love lost between me and Jack either. I'm jealous of Nibbler. He can growl and bite people he doesn't like on the ankles. I'd get locked up if I did the same thing."

"Was Jack in here?"

"No, he just walked past with a brunette, headed for Scottie's, I reckon." Noah shrugged as he moved Nibbler to one of his arms.

"A brunette?" Sam turned her head to glance back at the front of the store as if they'd still be visible.

"Yep." Noah sighed, picking up a few books with his left hand and walking them back to his main work desk in the center of the room as he continued, "One day, Kara's gonna see Jack for who he is. It ain't like he hides his running around. Everybody in Homestead knows about it, but no one can seem to talk a lick of sense into Kara when it comes to Jack. She's head over heels 'til he just up and vanishes for a weekend, then she goes off the deep end at Scottie's or at her mama's 'til he comes back. By Monday, he is slinking back in and buying her flowers. And just like clockwork, she takes him back every time. Kathleen calls those two the official H.S.O."

"What's that stand for?" Sam moved closer to the desk he stood at and leaned her hip against the corner of it as she listened.

"Homestead Soap Opera." He smirked, but the smile quickly fell from his face. "I feel for Kara. It's a messed-up cycle she's caught in. It's been said that you don't love what's good for you, you love what you know. Her daddy wasn't good to her mama when he was alive, according to the town chatter. And her mama's sick now, up in the oncology ward in Linden. When she is there visiting her, Jack brings girls down to that hunting cabin on the back end of Kathleen's property. The examples of love we experience as children influence us more than I think most of us realize."

Sam thought of her parents, their marriage of nearly fifty years, and the watertight bond they had. If that saying was true, how and why the hell did she ever fall for Chase?

Nibbler started to growl and wiggle in Noah's arms for the second time that evening when a tall, slender blond-haired woman came through the front door. Sam thought instantly of the movie *The Stepford Wives*, then *The Devil Wears Prada*. This sleek woman was the spitting image of the perfect trophy wife in her camel-colored, pin-tailored slacks, thin beige sweater, and high heels with the signature red soles all the sassy female lawyers in TV shows wore. Not a single blond hair was out of place, and her striking blue eyes narrowed in on Sam's dirty Adidas sneakers before looking her up and down in a measured way, ending on Sam's messy bun piled on top of her head. The Stepford wife look-alike pulled her mouth into a tight-lipped smile.

"Hello. You must be the redhead I have heard so much about." Laura's niceties tasted like fake sugar, leaving an odd taste in Sam's mouth.

"I guess I am. My name is Samantha," she said, straightening from the desk she had been leaning on.

"Laura." She pushed out her hand to take Sam's in a firm but perfunctory handshake before letting go like Sam's hand was a hot plate.

"If you're smart, you won't stay in this hellhole long," she said matter-of-factly and focused her attention back on Noah. "I'm cooking tonight. Don't lose track of time and be late. And since when did you start letting dogs in the shop? You know I'm allergic."

Sam's gut screamed at her that now was a pretty optimal time to excuse herself and leave, but her feet seemed to be soldered to the wooden floor where she stood. Nibbler was still growling down deep in his throat while Noah held him in his arms—and her book was in the back room. So was the tote bag she was supposed to fill before heading home. Being stuck somewhere between a rock and a hard place seemed pretty cozy to Sam right then.

Noah shrugged almost sheepishly. "There's exceptions to every rule. How about I grab a bottle of wine for dinner this evening?" he asked, changing the subject from Nibbler. "Red or white?"

"Both," Laura answered flatly.

"So, do you live here in Homestead?" Sam asked Laura, determined to act normal, though she could feel the distaste oozing out of Laura's every pore.

Laura scoffed and flipped her hair over her shoulder, and her eyes flicked back to Sam. "Not just no, but hell no. I live in Jefferson. I'm the judge's assistant at the courthouse there. What did you do before you came here?"

Sam was tempted to tell her some fantastic tale, just to see how high Laura's thin blond eyebrows could rise before disappearing into her perfectly styled hair. The thought of telling her the truth crossed her mind for a second, but she refrained. "A little of this and a little of that."

Laura gave a bored, "Hmm . . ." with a nod and looked back at Noah.

She figured that Miss Prissy Britches wasn't really interested in her past, and even if she was, Sam didn't give out personal information to people Nibbler hated.

"Like I said, don't be late," Laura said, her eyes darting back to Sam for just a moment before lasering in on Noah again.

"I won't be," Noah confirmed.

"I'm headed to my place, then. I can feel my allergies acting up already, I'm not giving you a kiss when you're holding a dog," Laura said with a look on her face like she stepped in something and was scraping it off her shoe. "Take a shower before you come over. And use a lint roller on your shirt and pants. I can't stand dog hair in the house." She dragged out the words *dog hair* like it was a dirty pairing of words.

"I'll do my best to get all the dog off me," Noah said without even looking at her.

Laura flipped one side of her hair over her shoulder and walked back to the door without a second look at Sam or another word to Noah. The thrumming *click-clack* of her heels on the worn wooden floor echoed after her and pounded in Sam's ears like the staccato rhythm of her heartbeat. When the door chime finally rang as she walked out, Sam could've sworn Noah let out a sigh, his shoulders lowering a few inches.

Why did he let her treat him like he was a doormat? Who could be with a man like this and talk to him like that in front of a customer in his place of work? Sam didn't know Noah that well, but she could tell he deserved better than that.

He is a stand-up guy, a catch really, she fussed.

And you know all this from only being around him a few times, huh? Inez was back.

Shut it! I ain't asking for a wise sage's advice right now, Sam mentally fired back.

The reason finally dawned on Sam why Laura had ruffled her feathers so much. It wasn't her clipped tone or her nonchalant snobbery. Laura reminded Sam of Chase. He had called the shots, and Sam had been convinced she was lucky to just be included. She went along with it for years, all the time knowing in her heart that something was amiss. Yet she stayed through all the drunken fights and demeaning arguments until the proof was finally in flesh in front of her, in the form of her best friend naked on Sam's side of the bed, and she couldn't ignore it anymore. She had no right to throw stones—at Kara's situation or at Noah's.

Noah closed the door and locked it, then set Nibbler down on the floor. He silently stood at the door for a moment before turning back to Sam and searching her face. "You look like you are fighting some kind of inner battle."

"I am," she admitted. "Laura is beautiful." She blurted it out like a child confessing a crime.

"She is," Noah agreed as he went around the front desk again to cash out the register for the day.

"I guess I'll get out of your hair now. I'll just grab the tote bag and come back another day for their books." Her voice wandered off as she pulled on her light denim jacket.

"No, I got the time to help you fill the tote up real quick. We can tag team and do it in no time. I'll empty the tote now and you go look. Kathleen normally gravitates to the back three shelves, and Loretta only looks at those two shelves there for her fix." He pointed out where Sam should look and got to emptying the bag. "Aim for two or three books for each of them. That'll keep them busy for a week or so. How many do you wanna take home?"

"Me?" she asked.

"Sure," Noah answered. "Since you live at Rose Garden, you can have the same borrow-and-bring-back deal that the others up there get."

"Well, thank you so much." She stopped scanning shelves for a moment, looked at him, and a genuine smile crawled across her face. "I think I'd like to branch out to some women's fiction with a hint of romance. What do you suggest?"

Noah pointed at the shelf toward the front of the store. "You should find a small but solid selection right there."

Sam was halfway across the room when she stopped and slapped the side of her leg. "Crap, Noah. I meant to bring your tie and flashlight to you, and I forgot."

"No problem at all," Noah said. "You can keep them or return them another time. This isn't the last time you'll be in the store, is it?"

"Nope, you now have three bookworms at Rose Garden in your lender program. I'm honored to join the ranks." Sam picked out three books for herself and added one each of that genre for Kathleen and Loretta. She worked her way down the shelves and soon had nine books stacked up in her arms. "Thank you, Noah. This is generous of you to let us read and return. I solemnly swear to not dog ear a single page."

"Shh . . ." His golden-brown eyes sparkled. "The town has ears, and if it gets out that I'm running a library, everyone will want the same deal. I only do this for a select few friends. As in the three who live at the Rose Garden. Oh, and Ruth Jones down on Shiloh Road. She has become a voracious reader since her husband passed. I don't know if you've met her just yet. She's a lot like Kathleen and Loretta. You'd like her."

"Well, then, I hope I meet her one day." Sam set the books on the desk and made a motion to zip her lips and toss the imaginary key over her shoulder. "As far as your secret lending program, the vault is sealed, and your secret is safe with me. Do I need to list the books?"

"I'll do it." Noah picked up a pen and notebook. "I have to keep a record in case those books are listed online for sale. I'll be here for another thirty to forty minutes probably. If you want to stay and keep reading in the back room till I go to close, you're welcome to."

"That sounds so tempting, but I'd better get on back to the B&B. The ladies are probably waiting on me for supper," Sam answered.

"Next time, then," Noah said as he put all the books into the bag. "It's getting dark. Do you need another flashlight?"

"Thanks again, but Nibbler and I can make it before it gets fully dark. Poor little guy has gone back to his chair and curled up for another nap. I almost hate to wake him." She went to the back room and hooked the leash on the dog's collar. "Okay, lil fella. It's time to go home. You've napped long enough."

Nibbler hopped down, all full of life and vigor again, and he rose up on his hind feet to do his cute little dance. That's when Sam realized that Noah was standing in the archway with a couple of treats in his hand.

"You and Kathleen are spoiling him."

"And having fun doing it." Noah gave the dog the treats. "I'll be interested to know if the ladies like the women's fiction books."

Sam picked up the tote bag and slung the wide strap over her shoulder and saluted Noah with a grin in mock ceremony. "I'll report back with my findings."

Sam was lost in her thoughts—Laura walking in and out of her mind—as Nibbler led the way up the hill, stopping several times to mark his territory. "If you ever want to do me a solid and pee on a mean woman's shoe, I promise to not yell at ya. Just aim for the red-bottomed ones," she muttered to Nibbler when he lifted his leg on the fence post as she opened the gate.

"Were you talking to me?" Kathleen popped up from behind a rose bush, and Sam let out a surprised squeak.

Kathleen placed a hand on her lower back and groaned as she stood and stretched. "I love this work, but it don't love me." Her face lit up when she noticed the tote bag, drooping heavily on Sam's left shoulder. "Let's go inside and see what you brought for us to read this week. The weatherman says we have a storm coming, and there's no reservations for next week. Do you know what that means?"

Sam shook her head.

"It means that Loretta and I need something to read in the evenings, or we'll bicker like old wet hens." Kathleen chuckled.

"We won't have cable for days if the wind's bad, and there won't be any cell service either. So, no *Green Acres* reruns for Loretta, and no going outside for me. That equals no peace for either of us. But I didn't say any of this to you." Kathleen turned to Sam as they neared the front porch. "Now, who were you talking to out there?"

"Nobody," Sam answered, her voice a little higher than normal—defensive even.

"Okay, then." Kathleen took her arm. "We'll have some hot tea and pound cake, and you can tell me what's got you all in a tizzy."

"I ain't in a tizzy!"

"And the sky ain't blue. Honey, I can read people as well as I can a book. What did Noah do?"

"Nothing, he didn't do anything," Sam finally admitted. "I just had the lovely experience of meeting his girlfriend, Laura."

"Oh, you've met the high-and-mighty Laura Henton." Kathleen snorted. "That girl's got a chip on her shoulder so big that I'm surprised she don't walk with a limp from the weight of it."

"What do you mean?"

"Laura came from humble beginnings. She was raised over in Pinecrest Properties, a trailer park just up a ways on the same road that the Rose Garden's on. Her mama has worked two jobs since Laura's daddy, J. W., just walked out one day and left them high and dry. Justine raised Laura on her own since she was real little. Her mama and them are good folks, but I think Laura was just so hell-bent on getting out of that trailer park and proving she was better than her upbringing, she forgot her manners somewhere along the way. When Noah's granddaddy passed, she locked in on Noah and figured that if she could become a Carter, then she could right her wrongs of being raised dirt-poor. She wants that name as much or more than his money. She can be as ruthless as Jack if she doesn't get her way."

Kathleen headed for the kitchen with her arm still locked in Sam's. "I hate to say that about Thurman's cousin's kid, but as Loretta says, 'he don't cull nothing.' Jack is always looking for his next conquest. And Laura's looking for her next victory to brag about. You can bet your last penny, she would leave Noah in a hummingbird's heartbeat if another man came along and could give her more, but she's got her eye on the prize and her claws in Noah so deep now, she probably ain't never letting him go." She let go of Sam's arm as they entered the room and put on the kettle without missing a beat. "She didn't have the easiest upbringing, but she was raised by a good Christian woman. Justine can't help it if life dealt her a hard hand."

"Why doesn't she like her family name?"

Kathleen shrugged as she pulled mugs from the upper cabinet and placed them to the left of the kitchen sink. "There's a few drunks in her family, and her dad was one of 'em. She cut contact with him when he moved farther west with a woman he met while still married to her mama. Justine still lives in the same single-wide that Laura was raised in, and I think it bothers her that she can't outrun or rewrite her childhood here in Homestead. Justine did her best with Laura, just as I did with my boys."

With mugs lined up beside the stove and the kettle going, Kathleen turned and stared at Sam with hawk-eyed scrutiny. "Now, let's talk about why she upset you today. We can't give all the credit to uppity Laura Henton, can we?" She refilled Nibbler's water bowl and dumped more food in his dish. "Poor little darlin' is probably wasting away after that long journey on such little legs. Ain't that right, lil bit?"

The way that Nibbler chomped away at the food bowl near Kathleen's feet, Sam guessed she was right. Sam's stomach growled when Kathleen pulled a lemon-glazed pound cake from the other side of the butcher block, took a long cake knife out of the drawer near her hip, and cut a slice for Sam.

"I wouldn't know where to begin, Ms. Kathleen," Sam said.

"I'm just Kathleen to you by now, honey. How about we start here?" Kathleen put a slice of cake on a paper plate and slid it in front of her with a fork. "Once upon a time, Samantha met a man . . ." Kathleen told her.

Sam barked out a pained laugh and almost choked on her first bite of pound cake. It was moist and buttery, but her mouth was as dry as the Sahara desert. She recognized the taste of lime instead of lemon in the sugary glaze.

The kettle sent forth a shrill whistle that sounded similar to the alarm bells ringing in her ears, and Kathleen pulled it off the lit burner. "There's a certain type of sadness only a man can put on a woman's face, and as someone who has seen that same expression in the bathroom mirror many a time, I know what I'm talking about. Rest assured, honey, I'm speaking from experience, so spit it out."

Kathleen put a chamomile tea bag in each of their mugs, leaving a third mug out presumably for Loretta, and poured the piping hot water into both before sliding one in front of Sam's plate.

"I haven't told you what brought me here, or what I was running from back home." Sam felt sick.

Kathleen poured a dollop of whole milk in her mug and left the red-topped gallon jug she had taken from the fridge on the butcher block table between them. "Some stories need to wait till the right time to tell." She picked up her fork and went on, "Loretta and I have some stories to tell you one day too. All strong women have backstories."

Sam let the floodgates open, and through tears and sobs, she told Kathleen everything about Chase and Liza Beth, from the beginning of their relationship to the ugly ending. "When I found them naked in our bed, I could've killed him. I really think I could've shot him dead if I'd had a gun." Her throat closed off, and she couldn't utter another word.

Kathleen sucked in a lungful of air and let it out in a whoosh. "I understand that feeling and the emotions around that kind of betrayal. And with your best friend?"

Sam nodded. Her eyes burned as she tried to stare a hole through the steaming cup of tea in front of her. She focused at the small chip on the side of the coffee mug, a splintered half of a painted rose that had flecked off from past use. She blinked away the tears collecting on her lower lashes. She couldn't seem to find her voice.

"Well, Sam, that's enough to make any woman see red," Kathleen continued. "I'm glad you didn't kill him and drove here instead, even if Patsy gave her life for the journey." She spun a spoon around in her mug, making circles in the milky liquid. "The past only has the power to define you if you let it, Sam. Sometimes, hard heartbreaks must happen to move us where God's wanting us to be. Every day that you let yourself think back on that betrayal and you let it eat at you is another twenty-four hours that those two no-goods have power over you. You can't move on and heal if you're hanging on to the past with a choke hold."

"But how do I move on? How the hell do you let go?" Sam hated the desperate note in her voice.

"It's not easy, but you pray for them."

"Pray for those two!" Sam gasped. "I think God would frown upon me asking Him for forgiveness for somebody that I still can't forgive."

"Well, I can't say I know exactly how God works. But there's a Mother Teresa quote I remember reading a while back. Someone asked her how she can see so many sick people day in and day out and not feel the weight of the world and all the suffering souls in it. Her response was beautiful. She said, 'I love them, I bless them, I pray for them, and I let them go.' I may be paraphrasing, but I say it all to make my point, and that is you can't hold on to heartbreak and heal from it." Kathleen craned her face to the kitchen ceiling and hollered, "Hey, Loretta! Come on down here. Sam's brought our books back and you need to hear this."

The lift squeaked like a mouse the size of King Kong as it lowered from the second floor to the first.

Loretta pushed back the black wrought iron gate and headed over to make herself a cup of tea, grabbing the extra mug from the counter and turning the kettle back on. "I'm all ears. What's going on?"

"Tell her," Kathleen said with a nod.

Sam repeated what she had told Kathleen. "And now Kathleen says I should pray for them, but I think I may get hives if I do so."

Kathleen focused on Loretta with an impish smile on her face. "Oh, I have faith you'll survive. The best of cures taste the worst going down. Retta, I think we need to hold hands and for you to lead us in one of your prayers."

"Give me a minute to get my tea made and sit down. My prayers don't go past the ceiling when I'm praying on aching feet." She finished what she was doing and then eased down in a chair across from Sam. "Alright, I can speak to God while my tea steeps." She held out her hands.

"We have to make a circle," Kathleen explained, "and you have to really want to get over the past for it to work, Sam."

Sam swallowed hard and nodded as she took Loretta's hand in her left one and Kathleen's in her right.

Loretta bowed her head and closed her eyes. "Lord, we are here today to ask that you help our sweet little friend move on from her ugly past. Help her to realize she is better off without a cheating bastard of a boyfriend or a bitch of a best friend. Keep her here in Homestead with me and Kathleen until she finds peace. I know that you are very busy, but if you could make Liza Beth get fat and ugly, and Chase go bald and broke, we would be very happy and very grateful. Amen."

Sam started to giggle and then threw her head back and laughed so loud that Nibbler thought she was crying and came over to whine at her feet. She picked him up but couldn't stop laughing as the dog licked at her face. "Well, I gotta say, I have never prayed quite like that, Loretta. I like your prayers," she said between the laughter induced hiccups.

"I told you if you prayed for those sorry bastards that it would make you feel better," Kathleen declared.

"My prayers have helped Kathleen a lot of times," Loretta said with a grin. "Someday we'll tell you all about Thurman, her dearly departed husband. There's a juicy story of redemption right there. Kathleen, hand me that fork."

CHAPTER FOUR

CLEOPATRA

S am dressed in charcoal gray slacks, a dark green blouse, and slipped her feet into her favorite pair of soft gray suede high heels. She checked her reflection in the long antique mirror and caught a glimpse of a calendar hanging on the wall behind her. She had arrived in Homestead on Valentine's Day, and it was already the last day of March.

"Well, now," Kathleen said from the foyer as Sam walked down the curved oak staircase, "don't you look nice!"

"Thank you." Sam smiled. "So do you."

When there were guests at Rose Garden, Kathleen wore jeans and a T-shirt, one step above her preferred outfit of well-worn bibbed overalls and torn flannel shirt when the roses were calling to her. That night, she had chosen a black power suit with a lovely gold rose brooch pinned to the lapel. Sam was still learning Kathleen, but she knew that when Kathleen wore her black suit, she meant business.

"Tonight, I'm the mayor, so I have to be presentable." Kathleen chuckled.

Loretta came from the kitchen with a silver tray of cheese straws in her hands. "I'm not anyone special, but I dressed up anyway." She had topped a flowing multicolored skirt with a bright orange blouse, belted at her tiny waist with a wide orange ribbon. Her matching earrings clinked as she swished around the room, setting up snacks and swiping imaginary dust off the occasional surface as she went.

"Y'all both look amazing," Sam said. "What can I do to help?"

"Greet folks at the door and send them into the living room," Kathleen answered. "Everything else is ready to go. Most of them have been here before and already know where to go."

"Do you always have city council meetings here?" Sam asked.

"Only a couple of times a year," Loretta answered. "The rest of the time we hold them at the church, but there's a wedding going on tonight."

Folks started to file in as the meeting approached. Some headed to the dining room for refreshments. Others went directly to the living room and found seats on one of the settees or claimed one of the folding chairs that Loretta and Sam had hauled up from the basement and had set up around the room.

"Good evening, everyone." Kathleen raised her voice. "It's time for us to begin this meeting."

She gave them a few minutes to quiet down and for the stragglers to take their seats. "The main focus of our meeting tonight is to discuss the Easter egg hunt and gather donations for the plastic eggs and candy to fill them," Kathleen said. "And we'll need volunteers to help stuff them. Donnie Stapleton, can I depend on you for your usual five hundred donation?"

"Of course," an older man dressed in a suit and tie said from the back of the room. "The bank is glad to donate to the cause."

A tingling down deep in Sam's heart told her that Noah was nearby before he even nudged her arm with his elbow. "Sorry I'm late, I had a last-minute customer who could talk the ears off a brass monkey."

I'm not attracted to a taken man. I am definitely not attracted to a taken man, Sam repeated as she scolded herself and straightened her shoulders.

"Noah, I see that you made it," Kathleen said.

"Better late than never," he said with a wave. "As always, I'll make sure there is plenty of candy to fill the eggs."

"I'll chip in another five hundred to be sure that we have plenty of eggs," an older lady with ink black hair said. "Last year there were so many kids that some of them only had one or two in their baskets. Our little event has started drawing children from Linden and Jefferson and all in between."

At that moment, the front door opened and closed with a loud bang. Nibbler let out a warning bark at the entry of someone new. The click of stiletto heels on the heart pine floors grew louder as Laura rounded the corner and made her grand entrance.

Her eyes skipped over Noah's face before landing on Sam's face right beside him and shooting a dirty look toward her before she turned back to Kathleen.

"Seems I got here in the nick of time. I have an idea I want to float."

"Let's hear it," Kathleen said, gesturing for Laura to come up front to talk.

"I vote that we have the egg hunt on Saturday at the same time the other towns have theirs. That way we won't get a lot of over-flow, and . . ." She glanced around the room and paused.

Sam was pretty sure that Laura was checking for anyone that might be nodding in agreement. If that was the case, then the woman was definitely disappointed, because all eyes had turned toward Kathleen.

After a pregnant moment, Laura went on, "We wouldn't have to gather as many donations because kids from other towns wouldn't be showing up out of the woodwork. So, I say we vote. All those who agree, raise your hand."

"Whoa! Whoa! Whoa!" Loretta popped up on her feet. "We're not going to vote that fast. All y'all need time to think about Laura's proposal. This has been Homestead's tradition since the first year when we started having the community egg hunt. We should leave the floor open for discussion for at least five minutes before we put it to a vote."

"I, for one, like to keep our traditions as they are and not change them, but I'm going to let y'all discuss Laura's idea before we make a decision," Kathleen said.

"Five minutes or five hours wouldn't be enough time to think about changing a tradition that goes back to when I was a little boy," the guy in the suit said. "I make a motion that we table Laura's suggestion until next year. Then we can bring it back up again and see how everyone feels."

Sam glanced over at Noah. His eyes were closed as if he would rather be anywhere in the world but in that room. She suspected Noah was in a tough spot. If he didn't agree with his girlfriend, she could and probably would give him the cold shoulder until she got her way. If he did agree with her, he would be sacrificing his own opinion to make her happy and going against what the whole town seemed to want. She didn't envy his situation.

"Let's vote on Donnie's idea to table this for a year," Loretta said. "It's not even three weeks until Easter, and I've heard a lot of folks have already planned their afternoon around the egg hunt."

"All in favor of revisiting this maybe in January of next year to give the people more time to make plans, raise your hand," Kathleen said.

Every hand in the room went up—except Laura's. Daggers shot from her eyes as she surveyed the sea of raised hands. She narrowed her eyes at Kathleen and then stormed out past Noah and Sam to the foyer.

Sam whipped around when Nibbler's growl was cut off by a yip of genuine pain out in the hallway. The poor boy was cornered near the front door, and Laura's foot was pulled back and aimed at him for what must be a second kick.

"Hey!" Sam bellowed so loud that everyone turned to look at her.

Laura swung around, and Nibbler scampered away from her. Her high-heeled shoe came down so heavy that it sounded like a shotgun blast on the hardwood floor. She pointed at Sam, then jerked her finger around at Nibbler, who had cowered near Sam and growled again. "You keep that filthy dog away from me. You don't belong here, neither does he."

Sam took a step forward and bowed up like a mama bear, moving closer until Laura's red-painted fingernail poked into her sternum. Her fists were clenched so tightly at her sides that her fingernails bit into her palms.

"If you ever kick my dog again," she whispered through clenched teeth, "I will shove my foot so far up your ass that every time you brush your teeth, you'll be shining my shoes."

"Don't you talk to me in that tone," Laura growled.

"You may be on a pedestal of your own making, but I don't have to bow down to you or even look up to you. However, if you ever want to come down to earth, I would be *glad* to help humble you."

"I'm leaving," Laura snapped. "But I'm telling you, if that dog ever growls at me again . . ."

"Don't say it unless you want to face the consequences," Sam said, grateful that Kathleen had control of the meeting, and no one was listening to the catfight in the foyer.

Flames sparkled in Laura's icy blue eyes. "Oh yeah? Well, *honey*," she said in a low growl that would have rivaled anything Nibbler could do, "when that old hag dies, I'm running for mayor, and I'm gonna run this town the way I see fit."

"Come on, Laura. I'll take you home," Noah whispered and stepped between the women and reached for Laura's hand.

"I can drive myself." She yanked her arm out of his reach. "You just stay here with all your *friends*."

Laura slammed the door behind her so hard the chandelier above Sam and Noah shook. The sound of her car tearing out of the driveway followed.

Noah turned to Sam with a hopeless look on his face. "I am so sorry about that. I don't know what got into her. You've been catching her on really bad days. She ain't always like this. I don't know where this came from."

"Alright," Kathleen's voice floated from the meeting. "Let's talk about prizes and a day to meet up to stuff eggs. Then we can end our meeting, and everybody can get home for dinner. Marvin, would your oldest boy, Wayde, be willing to be the Easter Bunny again this year at the egg hunt?"

"Of course," Marvin said.

Nibbler limped over to Noah and put both front paws on his knees. Noah crouched and pulled him gingerly into his arms. He checked his leg and hip by pressing around softly, watching the dog's face closely as he did. "I believe he's okay, but I'll be glad to take him to the vet in Jefferson first thing in the morning to be extra safe."

Sam sighed and watched Nibbler lick fervently at Noah's cheek as his sad golden-brown eyes scanned the dog's body, his hand still pressing around the dog's left hip. "Let's just wait and see."

"I'm sorry again. That was unacceptable. I will talk to her once she cools down a bit. Thank you for understanding." He looked like he wanted to say more, but he focused on Nibbler. "I'm sorry, old boy. I promise you will get every treat in the shop after this ordeal."

He gently handed him off to Sam. "I should get going. Tell Kathleen I've already ordered the candy, and it should be delivered next week. And tell her to put my name on the list to help stuff the eggs again this year. He stood up and dusted his pant legs off absentmindedly before looking down at Sam. "Again, I'm sorry. See you tomorrow, maybe?"

"I reckon so," Sam said with a nod. "Nibbler gets cranky if he doesn't get his evening walk each night. And I'm getting very spoiled getting that cozy little reading nook all to myself, and Loretta probably needs a new cowboy romance or two anyhow."

"You're a good person, Sam. I'm glad you came to Homestead." His smile couldn't erase the sadness in his eyes. He waved over his shoulder and disappeared outside.

Sam watched him on the path as long as she could by lamplight glow and then went back to the living room in time to hear Kathleen ask about prizes for the egg hunt. "In the past we've always given a bicycle to the winner in each group. What do y'all think about giving them a bag of books to encourage reading?"

"I like that idea," a woman on the sofa said, "but let's do both. A bicycle to the kid in each age group who finds the prize egg, and a set of age-appropriate books to the second-place winners."

"I'll sponsor the three bikes like I do every year," the man wearing a collared shirt with Gill Drugs embroidered on the chest piped in.

A lady in a blue hoodie with Homestead Produce emblazoned across the back raised her hand. "Put me down for the books. I'll talk to Noah to be sure which ones to buy."

Another guy's hand shot up. "I'll take care of a third-place prize for each group. My wife and I will give the child and their family a free dinner at the restaurant."

"Plus dessert?" Loretta queried.

"With ice cream," the lady who must have been his wife confirmed with a smile, and a soft chorus of chuckles bubbled around the room.

Nibbler lay sleeping in Sam's arms, his head tucked into the crook of her elbow as the meeting continued, a roomful of people working together to ensure the Easter festivities would be the best they could be for the kids in their town and the surrounding counties.

This whole town is cut from good cloth, Inez whispered in her mind. Sam agreed. Homestead wasn't just a town. It was an extended family that had gathered that night in Kathleen's home. By the time the meeting had ended, Sam's blood pressure was back to normal, even if she couldn't forget about Laura and her shitty attitude. She wondered if Noah was tracking Laura down to talk to her right now. What would he say to her? Every family tree has a few rotten apples, and Sam could spot one when she saw or smelled it—red-soled stilettos or not.

The next day, there was only one elderly couple staying at the B&B. The man and his wife had talked Loretta and Kathleen into playing canasta with them after dinner, so Sam snapped Nibbler's leash on him and headed out as Loretta cleared the dining room table for the card game. As spring pushed winter into the history books, the sun started setting later and later in the day, Noah kept the bookstore open until seven p.m., and she'd stop by most evenings. Sometimes she could only drop in for a minute or two, but if she had the time, she and Nibbler would escape to the back room to hole away in the softest chairs in Homestead. She would read as Nibbler snored.

That evening, Noah met them at the corner of the town square. "I was on my way to see about Nibbler. I was worried his leg was hurting him when I hadn't seen y'all yet."

"I think he'll pull through," she whispered as Nibbler recognized Noah and began dancing around his legs. "He was downright pitiful after you left, well, 'til Kathleen fed him all the sympathy treats he could eat before he almost barfed. I apologize for him for the way he acted with Laura. I don't know why, but he just seems to have a bone to pick with that woman. He does the same thing with Jack Reynolds."

Noah turned around and walked with Sam and Nibbler back to the shop. "He's got good reason not to like Jack," he said as he unlocked the door and held it open for them.

"And that is?"

He took a breath before answering her. "Jack ain't a good person," he answered and changed the subject. "I got a new box of romance novels in today, and it got me thinking. I've got a proposition for you."

"Oh, yeah?" Sam set the tote bag down on the floor beside the front desk.

"So, I was wondering . . ." he said, "would you be willing to write a short, one-paragraph review for some of the books you are reading? I could pay you a little bit for each one you write. Reviews help tremendously when selling books online. No pressure if you don't want to, just thought it might be fun for you to do, and it'd help me on the store's website."

Sam was so intent on listening to Noah that she didn't notice that Nibbler had woven a cat's cradle around her legs with his leather leash. She started to take a step but then realized that her legs were hog-tied. She let out a muffled *oof* as her head collided with Noah's collarbone. He wrapped his arms tightly around her and held her upright.

When she caught her breath, she reached down to untangle the leash from around her and unhook it from Nibbler's collar. She stood back up to see the strangest look in Noah's amber-colored eyes. Hunger, wariness, something so intense that Sam's cheeks started to burn. He pulled away abruptly and stuck his hands in his pockets, clearing his throat loudly and looking anywhere in the room except at her.

"Oh Lord, I'm sorry, I don't know how Nibbler even did that!" she said in a hoarse voice.

"I'm just glad you didn't bang your head on the corner of the desk. Kathleen would have my hide if I let you get hurt while you're here. And if you came back one night with a black eye or something, I can't even imagine what she'd do. Next time you'd see me, I could be the new rug in the dining room at Rose Garden." He grinned before looking away again and stepping back another step.

"Well, fret not. I survived. Your hide is safe from tanning for another day. Thanks to your quick thinking."

Why did her voice sound shaky in her head? *He feels the sparks between the two of you too.* The devil on her shoulder was giddy, hopping up and down, begging for her attention.

She brushed her shoulder off as if there were dust on it and shook her head. *Get thee behind me, Satan. I'm not a home-wrecker. I will not do what has been done to me. It was an awkward accident.*

"Yes," she blurted out.

"Yes, to what?" he asked, looking back at her face, confused.

"I'm agreeing to do reviews for you, but you don't have to pay me. I'll write them for getting to read the books without having to buy them," she answered. "It's a fair trade."

"Great! Pick out however many you want and whatever Loretta and Kathleen sent you down for, and I'll bag them up while you and Nibbler claim your favorite spot."

Sam inhaled deeply, loving the scent of the mixture of old books, the aged wooden floors of the shop, and—was that Stetson after-shave? She would have figured Noah would wear something far more expensive, but the smell brought her back to childhood. She used to dab the little tester bottles of perfume and cologne on her wrists and arms as a young girl, bored out of her mind at the Clinique counter with her mother in the local department store on Saturday afternoons. She once poured the whole bottle of Stetson's English Leather on herself by accident, then attempted to cover up her error by dousing the rest of her damp shirt in Miss Dior. She remembered her daddy asking her mama why their six-year-old smelled like a French bordello when they got home that afternoon and Wanette laughing and making Samantha explain. The whole house smelled like Stetson for a week even after Wanette washed her clothes a third time.

She had never picked up the scent of cologne in the shop before, only the warm tones of old paper and sawdust, coffee and cedar. But then, she had never been as close to Noah physically as she had been today in his arms.

"You should have a company create candles to capture the aroma of this place," she said, focusing back on the room, not the man in front of her.

Noah nodded toward the front of the store. Candles, cute little wooden signs about book lovers, and even a few T-shirts embellished with Mark Twain and Jane Austen quotes lined several shelves. "Good idea, but it's already been done. I sell a lot of that stuff around the holidays, or during the tourist season, which will be coming up real soon. There's a jar candle up there that really does smell like old wood floors and used books."

"Tourists travel all this way back into the woods?" Sam asked.

"Oh, yes, they do. They go to Jefferson for all the antiques stores, but they make the trek over here to wander through the stores on our historic town square. You've been to all the shops now, haven't you?"

"Not yet. I rode into town with Jack, and from what I could see, his auto business and a bunch of stores between there and here were either empty buildings or closed for the day," Sam answered. "Right here is as far as I've really wandered, other than back to Jack's to say goodbye to Patsy. Speaking of Patsy, that was really sweet of you to come to her funeral. And to think to bring roses."

"I knew that you had to be hurting. Kathleen had said y'all were having a funeral, and I thought flowers might help." He shrugged, but his cheeks reddened just a touch. "But back to the tourist season, Kathleen and I are working on bringing more business back to Homestead. That's one reason we want to keep the Easter egg hunt on Sunday. We've already talked all the stores on the square into staying open from two to five on that day so the folks who bring their kids to the hunt can spend some time here."

The bell above the door rang, and Sam took a couple of steps toward the reading room and grabbed Nibbler as he attempted to scurry past her to greet the folks walking in.

"Good evening, Kara, Rita Jo. Y'all lookin' for something in particular?" Noah asked.

Sam made a sharp turn to her left and pretended to suddenly be very interested in the paranormal romance section. She lingered in earshot. She had already seen Kara's face (and most of her body for that matter) on Jack's phone, but she wanted to hear her voice.

"Cowboy romance," Kara said.

"I'm thinking more thriller or gothic horror for me," Rita Jo answered and then followed Noah's finger across the room.

Kara cocked her head to one side and raised her voice, "Hey, are you the new girl in town? The one working for Kathleen at the inn?"

Sam wanted to pretend she was deaf, but she turned around and answered Kara, "Yeah, I'm Samantha. How did you know?"

"Jack told me that he hauled in an old Mustang a while back and that the driver was a redheaded woman who got a job working up at the Rose Garden," Kara answered. "Welcome to Homestead, Samantha. I'm Kara."

"Thanks, nice to meet you." A guilty flush washed over Sam.

Kara seemed nice, so why was Jack cheating on her? He and Laura should get together and make each other miserable instead of taking it out on nice people. She waved a little goodbye to Kara before slipping into the back room with her newest book and Nibbler in tow where she eased down into her regular chair. Nibbler had seemed unfazed by Kara and Rita Jo when they came in, wagging his tail instead of growling. Sam took that as a good sign.

* * *

After work on Thursday, Sam refreshed her makeup, spritzed perfume on her hairbrush—just a hint—and put on a white long-sleeved T-shirt with a sketch of a bookshelf, laden with books and the words *I Have No Shelf Control* printed on the front of the shirt. Liza Beth had given it to her for her birthday, but she'd never worn it until that very evening.

"You know you're going to have to donate your mess of books to the library if you get married. Chase wouldn't put up with all that junk lying around," Liza Beth had said when Sam opened the box and held the shirt up to her chest. Until that very moment, she hadn't realized that Liza Beth had said *if* you get married, not *when* you get married. What a difference one tiny little word could make.

Sam had found out later that Liza Beth and Chase had been sleeping together for a few months at that point. On the morning of her birthday, Chase was in a particularly cheery mood, saying he had to go out for something *very important* and would be gone most of the day. She had hoped he was about to propose and was buying her an engagement ring.

But he came back with candy in a bag from the gas station and some lotto tickets as her gift. "You're hard to buy for, so I just grabbed this."

She noticed his hair was a little damp when he got back to the house, like he had been caught in the rain or had recently showered.

When she got to the bookstore, Noah looked up and smiled, and just like that, Sam was back in the present and rerouted off memory lane.

"Hey, I like your shirt!"

"Thanks, I almost burned it. It's growth for me to wear it. Kathleen has sent me on a mission of forgiving and forgetting.

This is my first step," Sam replied, pulling the shirt wide and looking down at it.

"I hear a story in that statement," Noah said and glanced down at the folded-up paper in her hand. "Wow, you got a review ready for me already?"

"Not quite yet, this is a list from Kathleen. In this week's bag of books, there was one called *The Concubine*, a book about Anne Boleyn and King Henry. Now she wants me to see if I can find any nonfiction about other strong women throughout history. She's on a kick, and this week she seems really interested in Cleopatra. One of her friends from Jefferson told her a story of Cleopatra saving Egypt from invasions using roses and some quick thinking, so of course, the owner of Rose Garden now must do research and find out if it's a true story."

"Well, now I got to know what story this is, do tell," Noah replied as he shuffled books on his desk in front of her.

Sam laid the list on the counter and looked around the shelves as she started, "The story goes that when Cleopatra was pharaoh of Egypt, she got word that Rome was planning an invasion and quickly told her sailors to untie the masts and dip all the sails in rose water before hanging them again. They filled those same ships with roses and set off to Rome, surprising Marc Antony and the Roman Empire when they arrived with the smell of roses wafting in on the wind as they docked in the harbor. Marc Antony gave her a room in the royal palace as is customary for any traveling royalty, and that night Cleopatra set her trap. Her servants filled her room with rose petals, so many rose petals that they went up to their knees. She sent a letter, inviting Marc Antony to her chambers, where Cleopatra lay naked on a bed of roses as he entered. They got it on, and Cleopatra made Marc Antony promise that he would never invade her country as long as she was pharaoh. She said she filled the room with roses, so that from then on, anytime Marc Antony smelled a rose, he would remember their union and their agreement. They turned out to be great lovers, according to Kathleen." She grinned at Noah. "For her sake, I hope it's true. It's a cool story."

Noah raised his eyebrows and shook his head. "Well, that was like a chess move in a game of checkers. I love it when Kathleen gets on a new kick—I learn more about what I have in this shop every time she does. I'll look on the computer and see what books we have on Cleopatra now." As Noah leaned over the ancient computer behind his desk and scrolled down the titles, Sam scanned the bookshop silently, letting her thoughts wander from one thing to another.

"You know, I've been to a lot of used bookstores, and the new rage seems to be organizing some sections by mood as well as genre."

"How would I do that?" Noah asked.

She unsnapped Nibbler's collar and he meandered through the shop, checking out every nook and cranny as Sam slowly walked from one aisle to the next to look, talking louder the farther she got from his desk so he could still hear her. "I don't think it'd be too hard. It would just be a sorting job. You have historical romance books in this section. If you broke it down and put sub-labels on the shelves—like dark medieval or sweet Victorian—then your customers would know the mood of the book. I could help you since I know more about the romance book realm than you do, Mr. Nonfiction."

"I could use help in the romance section, for sure. Cowboy romances seem to be the latest craze online and in town. And from what I've surmised, they range from wholesome to straight up raunchy. Maybe the cowboy section could be divided into three sections: bedroom door closed, bedroom door slightly ajar, or bedroom door wide open and beyond." Noah grinned and slid a sly wink across the room.

Is he flirting with me? Sam wondered. *Or am I just imagining the playful lilt in his voice just then?* She stooped down behind a row of shelves, using the books for cover, and pretended to study the titles to keep him from seeing her blush.

The flush drained from her face when the sound of a loud siren screeched and Nibbler threw back his head and howled. She came around the corner of the science fiction section in time to see her dog making a mad dash to Noah, trying his best to jump up into his arms.

"Poor little guy." Noah picked up the dog and held him close to his chest. "I'm sure that hurts your ears, but it means that we need to take cover. A tornado is headed this way, and we need to get down in the basement."

"Wait? What basement?" Sam asked. "A tornado for real?"

"Noah nodded at the phone near his head and fished out two flashlights from a lower desk drawer and then opened a door to the right of his desk. "Call Kathleen and tell her that you're safe. Be quick though. The police station doesn't blow the warning siren unless they've seen a tornado close by."

Sam hated cellars and basements—any room with no windows, really—but she had seen the destruction that a tornado had left behind just south of Jefferson a few weeks before. She called Rose Garden, and Kathleen answered on the second ring and sounded out of breath. She told Kathleen she was safe, then hung up and called her parents. The alarm seemed to be getting louder or closer somehow. She nervously tapped her foot and held her breath as the phone rang five times, each ring seeming to be longer than the last. Her father's voice on the machine finally answered, so she left a message.

"Hey, don't worry. You are hearing the tornado warning in the background. I don't know what you'll see on the news later tonight or tomorrow, but I want y'all to know I'm fine. I'm heading into the basement now. I love y'all, I'll call as soon as I can." She hung up the phone and closed the door behind her on her way down the steps.

"Welcome to the Cellar Lounge, a speakeasy from the 1920s during prohibition," Noah said from his seat on a futon against the back wall with Nibbler in his lap. He patted the empty space beside him. "Sit down, and we'll all three ride out the storm together."

"You know that old song, 'Storms Never Last'?" Sam asked as she eased down onto the futon and scanned the room. The place was every bit as big as the bookstore, and it had been kept in pristine condition except for the modern-day futon they sat on and a bit of dust on the gorgeous, shiny mahogany bar stretched across one end with an antique mirror behind it. All that was missing was barstools and bottles of liquor lining the back shelves. A time capsule, hidden under a bookshop, seemingly untouched by today's world.

"Where's the moonshine?" she asked.

He leaned his head back against the cement wall behind the futon and stared at the ceiling. "To answer your questions, I don't think I've heard that song since my grandfather died. I rarely drink, so I sent all the booze up to Kathleen. I keep one bottle of whiskey in the bar, the kind my dad and grandfather loved, for sentimental sake."

"I'm surprised folks don't badger you to come down and see this. It's like taking a step back in history—it's so old-timey in here."

"Very few people know this place exists." Noah's eyes followed hers around the room as she took in everything. "It's sorta my little hidey-hole. I keep some extra clothing down here and sleep on this futon when there's bad weather. Now . . ." He turned to look at Sam. "Before the storm warning sent us down here, you said something about forgiving and forgetting when we were talking about your T-shirt. Is it a story you're willing to share? I won't lie. I'm sorta curious about how you landed in Homestead."

"It's a long story," Sam warned. Telling Kathleen and Loretta the other night had been cathartic, but that didn't mean it wasn't emotionally exhausting to recount and relive all the sordid details.

"Hey, you don't have to tell me anything if you don't feel comfortable. We gotta wait for the all-clear siren, and I don't know how long it might be before we can leave, so I just thought I'd ask. Don't worry, we can talk about something else." His kindness was the sort of thing that made a woman comfortable enough to confess everything.

"No, I'll tell you," Sam finally said after staring in his eyes for what felt like too long. "I'm learning to let it all go anyway. Maybe this is practice." She told him everything, how she got a scholarship to Nashville, then gave it up because Chase had said that he couldn't live without her. How they had broken up more than once, taking months away from each other sometimes, but he'd show up and win her back over and over again.

"The worst part wasn't giving up the scholarship out of state to stay in Rosepine for him. It wasn't the fights or the ugly breakups, but it was that he slept with my best friend. Or more, that my best friend slept with my boyfriend. I lost two people I loved when I found out." She looked down at her shirt and said, "That's why I almost burned this shirt. She gave it to me. Kathleen says I gotta let it go, but it's just hard, you know? The one person I wanted to call and cry to when I found out Chase was cheating on me, and was lying to me the whole time too, had been cheating on our friendship. So, I left. I just packed all my shit, and then my car broke down, and here I am."

"I can't imagine that pain, Sam. You are a strong person, stronger than you probably realize. Thank you for trusting me enough to tell me all that."

In that simple comment, Sam felt an overwhelmingly warm sense of safety. She was at home here with him, sitting on a stretched-out futon in a concrete basement as a siren screamed in the distance. She wondered if this was how things started between Liza Beth and Chase. Friendly conversation, all the small talk maybe being completely innocent, until a single gaze between them lingered just a tad too long. Did their hands accidentally touch, and sparks shoot between them, startling them both?

Liza Beth and Chase both worked at the bank in Rosepine. They ran into each other all the time five days a week. Maybe there was a moment in the vault, where space was tight and they touched, by accident at first, then maybe not by chance. She remembered Chase driving to Jefferson to buy cologne the Christmas before last. He had always said he didn't wear the stuff, but something and someone had changed. Did Liza Beth spray perfume on her hairbrush before work?

The thought was like a hot penny burning a hole clean through Sam's stomach. Because *she* had done that very thing, just this evening, before coming to the shop. She was a hypocrite if there ever was one.

"Yeah, well, thanks for listening." She was ready to hit the ball into a safer-to-navigate area of the court. "Now, it's your turn. Tell me how you and Laura met."

"We've known each other since we were in elementary school. We were in the same class but in completely different worlds. I was a nerd through and through and always had my head in a book. I don't think Laura knew I existed back then. She was the prettiest girl in town growing up. It wasn't until my grandfather died that . . ." He paused. "Maybe I should say it all started when he died. He was the last relative I had, and she showed up at the hospital. I was completely lost. I didn't know what to do. Laura stepped in and helped me get his accounts in order, and steered me through the funeral plans. I really don't know if I could've done all that without her guiding me through the grief I was still processing. Before I even realized it, we were dating and have been since then."

"Are we friends?" Sam asked quietly after a moment's pause.

Noah locked eyes with her. The soft light in the old speakeasy did nothing to dim the golden glint in his eyes.

"Of course we are," he answered.

"As your friend, then . . ." Sam paused. "Why do you let her treat you like she does?"

"She needs me." Noah's voice sounded weary. "When I had needed someone back then, she was there. She struggles internally with self-worth, with where she is in her life as well as in the world."

"Grew up on the wrong side of the tracks, right?" Sam said before she realized.

Noah nodded. "Yeah, and she can't seem to put it to rest. She just wants to be accepted, to be somebody in this small town to prove to everyone that she isn't that little girl from the trailer park wearing secondhand clothes. She worked hard in school, got a good education and her master's, has a great job now over in Jefferson, but in Homestead, she . . ."

"She still feels like the child from the trailer park who has to prove herself?" Sam asked.

"Exactly. Sometimes," Noah answered with a sigh, "I get the feeling that she's not truly happy being with me, but when I needed her, she was there for me. Now that she's having a hard time, I can't leave her high and dry. She deserves the kind of support she gave me."

Before Sam could think of anything to say, a secondary siren sliced through the night, and Noah slapped his hands on his thighs and stood up from the futon.

"And that ends our time in the Cellar Lounge for the night. I'm glad you and Nibbler were here to keep me company." He smiled down at Sam for just a moment before turning to the staircase. "Let's go see if we got any damage upstairs."

Nibbler was up the rickety staircase in a flash, pawing at the door until Noah opened it. Sam made her way to the front of the shop, looking at each window carefully to see if there was any damage done. After confirming all the windows were alright, she turned back to see Noah looking up at the ceiling, eyeing every corner for leaks.

"Good news, all the windows are A-OK. How are we doing up here?" She looked up too, crossing her arms over her chest.

"I think we survived unscathed." Noah smiled at her. "I'll call around and see if it touched down in town or if we're all in the clear."

Sam clamped the leash onto Nibbler's collar. "I should get going. Kathleen and Loretta might need help if the storm did any damage up there."

"Oh, of course." Noah opened the door and stepped out onto the sidewalk. "Looks like some big tree limbs are down. You sure you want to walk back, or would you rather me drive you up there?"

Sam took in the wet leaves and branches blanketing the rain-slicked road as Nibbler tugged at his leash. "We're good, thanks though. I feel like there's a different kind of stillness that settles in after a big storm like that. I find it calming."

Time alone to think was what she needed. And cold air on her face and space from the man with warm brown eyes and a good heart. Lots of space away from him.

"Okay, I'm gonna close up and head home too, then. Goodbye, Sam, and goodnight." Noah's tone seemed to hold a measure of wistfulness.

CHAPTER FIVE

BREAD AND BUTTER

The walk home wasn't as calming as Sam had hoped it would be. As she and Nibbler headed up the hill, she kicked small branches out of the path and tried to do the same mentally every time her mind wandered back to Noah. Nothing helped. Guilt hung like a wet weighted blanket around her shoulders.

The screech of the lift greeted her when she opened the front door, and Kathleen and Loretta hurried out of the kitchen—both panting.

"No damage upstairs. The basement is dry," Kathleen said on her way out the door. "I have to check the roses. Damn storms."

"There's one good-sized maple blocking the road. We climbed over it on the way here," Sam said, "but other than that, I think we're in the clear."

The fact that her cell phone rang surprised Sam, but she sat down on the first step of the staircase and answered, "Hey, Mama, how are ya . . ."

"Are you alright?" Wanette's worry was loud and clear in her voice even through the static. "We haven't heard a word about a tornado up in that area."

"Everything's fine," Sam assured her mother. "I was in the bookstore when the whistle blew. Noah and I rode out the storm in the basement." She went on to tell Wanette all about the old speakeasy.

"Uh, huh, that's good. When are you coming home?" Wanette finally asked.

"Two days after I quit being happy here," Sam answered. "Mama, I like the place. I'm making friends. I'm even saving up, and Buster, down at the auto shop, is looking at auction lots for me for a newer Mustang model."

"I don't like you being so far from home." Wanette sighed. "But you're a grown woman. And I learned a long time ago that you gotta do what you gotta do. You don't ever listen to me once you've made your mind up, anyway."

"I wonder where I get my hard head from?" Sam teased, and swore she heard her father's gruff laughter in the background before she lost connection again. "I love you, Mama, but I'm only catching half of what you're saying, my phone's going in and out. I'll call you back on the home phone in the morning, okay?"

"That's a good plan. Me and your daddy love you," Wanette said and ended the call.

Sam met Kathleen in the kitchen and dropped the books on the counter. "Your literary carrier pigeon has brought you some goodies. Noah found some more books about Cleopatra for you to gorge yourself on."

"Oh behold the great Queen Cleo! I'm gonna start with"—Kathleen grinned widely as she pulled a book out with Cleopatra's stone statue adorning the front—"this one."

"How are the roses? Did they lose a lot of blooms?" Sam sat down on a stool at the butcher block and rested her elbows on the weathered wood with her chin on her hands.

"They didn't suffer too bad," Kathleen assured her. "Speaking of something blooming, what is happening with Noah?"

"What about him?" Sam's voice caught at the sound of his name.

"Is there something brewing between y'all?" Kathleen asked.

"No! Of course not. He's with Laura, and I'm not a home-wrecker." Sam felt like she was a kid clutching a baseball mitt in front of a broken window.

You haven't done anything wrong, the little reassuring voice in her head reasoned, *yet*.

"Okay." Kathleen's tone suggested she didn't completely believe Sam.

"I would never do to anyone else what was done to me," Sam declared.

Kathleen nodded and dragged a stool to the other side of the butcher block and sat in front of Sam. "I know that you ain't the running around kind, but you get a certain light in your eyes when you're with him. And Noah seems to be keen on you too. I just wanted to make sure you weren't making a decision you would regret later on—that's all." She reached across the table and patted Sam's hand.

"We're just friends . . . That's all we are . . . and that's how we're keeping it," Sam stammered.

"Okay, honey. I'll hold ya to it." Kathleen left it at that.

"Yes, ma'am, and now I'm going to bed." She slid off the bar-stool and headed up the stairs to her room.

"I haven't done anything wrong; I haven't done anything to be ashamed of," she murmured as she clicked off the lamp beside the bed.

The darkness didn't seem to agree. After lying in her bed for what seemed like hours and chanting mantras to rid her thoughts of Noah, he met her in her dreams that night.

They were cooking supper in a whitewashed, cottage-style kitchen with a window over the sink. She didn't see him approach but rather felt him. Noah's arms slid around her from behind, his hand running along the curve of her hip and landing against the softer curve of her tummy. His lips hovered near her ear, she could feel his warm breath on her neck as his arms tightened and pulled her back against him. When his lips finally touched her neck, Sam bolted upright in her bed, blinking wildly, not knowing where she was for a moment.

She flopped back onto the bed and groaned as her alarm sounded: 8:01 a.m. She hurried to the bathroom, brushed her teeth, ran a brush through her hair, and then ran down the stairs. She needed coffee and conversation to get Noah off her mind.

"I hope that delivery boy gets here by noon," Loretta was saying when Sam reached the kitchen. "I got a half a dozen early orders of Easter lilies that must be delivered today or we're gonna catch hell on Easter morning."

Kathleen opened the back door for Nibbler. "We'll figure out something if we need to. I can chip in today if I need to, so don't worry, Rett, just drink your coffee." Kathleen returned and poured batter into a waffle iron. "I bet the First Baptist and Methodist churches would be fine with us dropping them off early in the morning if we have to."

Loretta grumbled at Kathleen as the older woman pulled a pan of scrambled eggs off the front burner. Loretta was already at the door, calling Nibbler in with her thermos in hand and purse in her arms. "I haven't got time for breakfast. I'll get an energy bar at the flower shop." She hollered her goodbyes and had disappeared before Sam made it to the coffeepot.

"Good morning, Sam. Noah called earlier." Kathleen flipped the waffle iron over. "He said he's changing his hours. He's gonna be closing the shop at five now. Laura wants him home earlier in the evenings, I reckon."

Sam's heart fell into her stomach. She gulped down coffee and headed to the shop, skipping breakfast and leaving Nibbler begging at Kathleen's feet. When she opened the back door, Loretta's bouffant hairdo bounced around from behind a beautiful bouquet. She added some baby's breath and stepped back to admire the huge arrangement. "What do you think?"

"It's stunning, Loretta. Is it for one of the churches in town? It's pretty enough to be a wedding arrangement." She reached out and softly cupped a white hydrangea, marveling at what masterpieces Loretta could create with just flowers.

"Nope. Noah put in the order the first thing this morning to be delivered to Laura at the courthouse. I asked him what the occasion was, and he said he just wanted to do something nice for her. He's a catch, that one."

"Oh." Sam felt like a rusty spatula scraped her heart off the bottom of her stomach and flipped it over onto burning coals. "Does Noah send flowers to Laura often?" she asked even if she didn't want to know the answer.

"No, I think he's more of a jewelry guy when it comes to buying for her. This is the first time he's sent flowers from here, so I tried to make it real nice." Loretta's smile said she was proud of her work.

"Are they ready to go?" Kathleen came through the back door with the keys to the delivery van in her hand.

"I just need to get them settled into the tote box," Loretta answered and nodded toward a book lying beside her. "Looks like we've got an easy day after all—at least until the delivery guy gets here with the lilies. Unless someone dies and we get a dozen or two orders for a funeral on Monday, I'm claiming that red chair in the back of the office, and I'm reading till closing time. Sam, you will have to entertain yourself until our flowers come in."

Today of all days, Sam would've given her left foot to be so busy that she couldn't think straight. Loretta helped Kathleen carry the tote outside while Sam stared a hole into a thick pad of sticky notes on the counter in front of her.

He must feel guilty. Why else would he send a giant bouquet to Laura if he had never done so before? Maybe ordering flowers for Laura was his subtle sign to Sam that he was indeed taken and off-limits. If Kathleen was observant enough to see her crushing on Noah, did he notice it too? He must have. Or Laura did. Or maybe everyone in Homestead knew.

"If you get tired of just standing there, there's a beanbag in the back," Loretta said when she walked in and found Sam in the same spot. "That was Vivian's napping corner. I can't count how many times I had to help her up out of it before she gave birth. That girl looked like she swallowed a watermelon near the end."

"Do you have kids?" Sam asked.

"No, darlin', I was married for a short while. I figured out pretty quick that I had hitched my wagon to the wrong horse. A mean old drunk horse."

"Kathleen was married for a long time, and she had two boys, right?"

"Two sons, the elder is Andrew, younger is Bubba. Well, we all called him that. Andrew moved to New Orleans. He's a chef down there. Bubba? Well, nobody knows what he is up to these days."

"Do they ever visit?"

"Heavens no. Those boys thought their daddy hung the moon. When Thurman died, they stopped coming around. Andrew calls on the holidays to check in on Kathleen. Bubba calls her when he needs some more money." Loretta fussed with the Oasis blocks under the counter until all the green squares were in a tidy stack. "Thurman poisoned them boys against Kathleen and then blamed Kathleen when the boys both left Texas. He was the kind of man who didn't have to drink to be vicious. He could do that pretty well when he was sober."

"I can't understand how a man could be cruel to Kathleen," Sam mused.

"A mean enough man will always be cruelest to the ones closest. You remember that." She looked back at Sam with a serious expression. "Kathleen will tell ya, neither of us have ever been good with picking men, but we're good with flowers. That's our calling— our bread and butter. I stick to what I'm good at, and I leave the rest for the other women in the world to figure out. I'm gonna order pizza for lunch. You want some?"

The abrupt change of topics now closes the door to that particular conversation, Sam thought and nodded.

Nibbler was sprawled out beside Kathleen on the chaise longue out in the backyard and didn't budge when Sam walked out with his leash in hand. Kathleen rubbed his head with one hand, a book in her other. One look from Nibbler told Sam that she was on her own tonight. She thought it odd that he would rather stay with someone other than her. That was a first.

"Looks like you'll be taking your walk alone tonight." Kathleen chuckled. "Don't worry. We are the best of friends now. Cleopatra and I will take good care of him. Oh, and if you see Marsha Hubbard at the candle shop when you go by, will you please tell her I have that order coming in first thing in the morning?"

"Of course." She went back in and picked up her purse, thought better of it and put it back, taking only the flashlight before leaving. She had meant to return it to Noah but never had. The heavy weight in her hand brought back memories of the night he gave it to her. The sparks that flew down her arm and through her body at the slightest touch of his fingers came back full force, and her stomach clenched. She should've never gone back into that bookshop. If she was a better person, she wouldn't have struck up a friendship with Noah after that. His cell phone number was written on a strip of duct tape on one side of the metal grip, almost rubbed off from the time the flashlight had lived in her purse. She twisted the handle until it was hidden in her palm.

The bouquet was her wake-up call. Between the mountain of snow-white hydrangeas and him changing his hours, her gut told her it was time to back off. After the hard talking-to and a few shed tears in the shower when she got home, she figured it was best for everyone involved if she stayed away from Noah—after she gave him back his property. She took off in a sprint, Noah's flashlight clutched in one hand, the other fist clenched as she ran down the hill. *I'm making the right decision*, she told herself for the thousandth time.

If I was Laura, this is what I would want. It's better this way. She repeated that over and over as her legs started to burn. When she reached the sidewalk's edge, she felt as if she were stuck at a crossroads. Her plan was to walk on the opposite side of the street after she either handed the flashlight to Noah or else left it in the mailbox. But the light flowing out of the bookstore's windows and pouring onto the sidewalk drew her like a mouse to a trap.

Maybe he changed his mind about updating the store hours.

The devil tap-danced on her shoulder and shrieked with glee. Music trickled through the storefront. Sam was drawn to the glow of the bookstore like she had been on the first night she arrived in Homestead. Before she realized she was about to go inside when she stopped herself. No, she couldn't go there anymore, she reminded herself firmly.

Put the flashlight in the mailbox and keep walking, or else go inside and see him just one more time. The devil was mighty convincing, and Inez was offering no quick retort to slap sense into her. Her hand was on the doorknob, but when she looked up, she let go as if it were scalding hot.

The new hours were written in cursive on a paper taped to the bottom of the CLOSED sign in the window. Right there in the middle of the bookshop, in front of the desk, Noah held Laura as they swayed to the music coming from an old radio. There was no mistaking that they were in love because Sam had seen her parents dance just like that. And there was no doubt they loved each other more than anything in the world.

Laura's head was on Noah's shoulder, and his hand cradled her back as they waltzed in slow circles. Laura threw her head back and laughed at something Noah said, and a bucket of cold clear reality dumped itself over Sam's head, waking her up. She staggered back from the door and quickly crossed the road, tears clouding her vision and blood pounding in her ears.

She ran until she felt like she might puke, stopping finally to bend over and heave in stilted breaths, her hands on her knees, tears hitting the pavement. One tear landed near a small dandelion at her feet, fighting its way through a crack in the sidewalk, and then another. Her grief watered the little straggler as her breathing slowed.

She wanted to call her mama, but she knew she couldn't, not yet. Her mama and daddy would be in the car and coming Sam's way before she could even explain the situation. And what would she tell her anyway? That she was this heartbroken over a taken man she had a crush on?

She wasn't ready to head back to the B&B because Kathleen would still be up and asking why Sam was so upset. She had just vowed to Kathleen last night that she and Noah were just friends. How could she explain her puffy face without Kathleen seeing straight through her?

The backs of her heels burned, blisters starting to form where her socks had slipped down. She wiped her eyes on her shirt sleeve and looked up and down the street. The candle shop was dark, and so was most of the street. The only place still open at this time of night was Scottie's.

A drink would help. The devil had run off Inez as well as the angel who normally resided on her other shoulder. She made a beeline to the barred window and peered in.

She counted four or five folks sitting at the bar, a couple on the dance floor, and another in one of the booths. No Noah. No Laura. No Jack either. Her hand was on the door handle and yanking it open before she gave the idea of going in or staying out another thought.

"Hey, Samantha!" Buster yelled across the room so loudly that the folks at the bar turned around to see who he was greeting. He and the pretty brunette by his side waved. "What are you doing here? I thought you spent your evenings at Noah's place with your nose in a book."

"Sometimes books get boring." She hoped that her voice didn't tremble as badly as her hands.

"Amen to that, but according to my wife, Allie, right here"—Buster kissed the woman on the top of her head—"they are the golden ticket during deer season. If I wanna go hunting, I know to make a stop at Noah's and grab enough books to keep her happy till I get back, don't I, baby?"

"It took me some time, but I have him trained real good now," the woman said with an impish grin and a wink at Samantha. "I'm Allie. Buster told me about your car. Oh, and your little pup! I want to meet him sometime. I love dogs, and Buster said he looked like he was some kind of terrier mix?"

"I don't really know what all he is. Jack called him a Heinz." Sam shrugged.

"Don't listen to him. He ain't a dog person. If he was, he'd know the best dogs are always mutts."

"Amen again," Buster agreed with Allie and took the final swig of his Miller Lite before pushing it forward on the bar to let the bartender know to bring another one.

"Rita cracked a new Miller Lite to slide Buster's way and yelled above the music on the jukebox, "Hey there, Red, welcome in! I didn't introduce myself the other day. I'm Rita Jo. What can I get ya?"

"A shot of Jack and a chaser of Coke, please." Sam paused. "Hey, is that booth taken?" The red vinyl booth against the wood-paneled back wall looked like the best hiding place in there to lick her wounds.

"It's all yours now, honey. Go on and have a seat. I'll bring your order over to ya." Rita poured and pushed a Guinness to one man to her left and handed an onion ring basket to a man at the other end.

Buster guided Allie back to the dance floor, and they started into a two-step again. For such a big man, Buster was smooth on his feet, and Allie followed his lead like a slim reed swaying in the wind. The image of Noah and Laura dancing earlier flashed in her mind and bit at her.

Rita Jo returned with a heavy-handed shot of whiskey and a tall glass of Coke with lots of ice. "I hope you meant you wanted it this way. I can mix 'em if this ain't what you meant."

"No, this is perfect. My daddy drinks it like this. He says that you shouldn't ruin good whiskey with a Coke, or good Coke by putting whiskey in it."

Rita Jo laughed at that. "Smart man."

"So, you like dark mysteries?" Sam asked.

"You remembered." Rita Jo beamed. "I was raised on the Brontë sisters and Nancy Drew. I never grew out of it, and it's always been my go-to." Rita propped her hip against the side of the booth table and leaned in a bit. "You know, word around town is that you practically live at Everbloom these days. Are you a book addict or just . . . you know, sniffing around?"

Sam almost choked on a sip of whiskey. The burn traveled all the way to her stomach before she answered, "No, no, I'm just a bookworm. I worked at the library back in my hometown, and I miss being around books all the time, that's all." Sam took another sip and chased it quickly with a swig of Coke. "News travels fast in a small town, doesn't it?"

"Yes, it does, but rumors travel even faster," Rita Jo said and then lowered her voice and stooped even closer. "The latest gossip in town is that you and Noah have a thing going."

"Sorry to disappoint the rumor mill but"—Sam finished off the shot in one gulp—"there's nothing going on between us other than just a shared love of books."

"Good, because I'd hate to have to whip your ass." Rita Jo's giggle was only half sincere. "Laura went to school with me and Kara. We still stay in touch even though she moved to Jefferson. We're hoping that she'll move back if Noah ever pops the question, so don't go getting in the way of our master plan." Sam wondered if it'd be a funny moment to tell the woman that she could probably deal an ass kicking back to her worse than she could give. Her dad had been a military brat himself and was now retired from the military and had decided that his children would know self-defense. Her sisters hadn't particularly enjoyed it, but Sam loved the classes she took every summer.

"Never crossed my mind," Sam assured her as she took a sip of her Coke.

"Well, holler if you need anything." Rita Jo eyed the empty shot glass. "You want me to go ahead and bring you another?"

"Thanks, but I'm a one-drink pony." Sam forced a smile.

She shoved the flashlight to the far side of the booth, leaned her head back against the wood paneling, and focused on thinking about anything but Noah, but she couldn't think of anything else. They had never held hands or kissed, so why did this ache in her chest feel so very visceral, like it might tear through her from the inside out? She was such a damn idiot. And a hypocrite. She was Liza Beth in a different font, and that made her feel icky. She tried to think of the men in Homestead, any man her age that wasn't Noah, but his brown eyes kept flickering across her mind like flies buzzing around a church buffet—always somewhere watching, never quite gone no matter how much you wished them to just leave you be.

The only men she met were guests at the Rose Garden, either on a newlyweds trip with their partners or headed through town on their way to somewhere else. Or the married men who would ring the flower shop for the occasional anniversary or funeral. She tried to rationalize the lump in her throat. She didn't fall for him because they had a special connection or anything. It was because he was the only nice guy around who was steady and her age.

That's it! Her brain greedily sank its claws into this explanation. She only liked Noah because she was a bit lonely and still grieving a past breakup. Homestead didn't offer many distractions for a wounded heart. And crushing on someone completely unattainable was her wounded heart's way of distracting itself from the loneliness.

She hadn't made it to Mena, so Homestead had to do. And she wasn't completely alone. She had Kathleen and Loretta, and as always, she had Nibbler. It was too soon to even think about going back to Rosepine, but if she really focused, she could move on from this silly crush on Noah and make Homestead work until she bought another car.

She was tired of running away from heartbreak. She had her dog. She had her books. But her brain snapped back to Noah like a tape measure slapping shut, and dammit if the heartsick pining brought his face back around to haunt Sam.

CHAPTER SIX

THE POT AND THE KETTLE

PART ONE

D on't let him come in here. Lord, please don't let him come in here," Sam whispered when a shadowy figure passed by the window and blotted out the stars. Jack Reynolds had this thing about him that she couldn't explain, but Sam knew it was him just from his shadow. He was a hard man to miss.

God must have sent her prayer to voicemail because Jack pushed open the door and strutted past the dance floor. He slapped a couple guys on the back as he approached the bar and winked at a sour-faced Rita Jo.

"Hey, Red," Rita Jo hollered over the noise, "do you want a refill yet?"

God hadn't heard the prayer, but it sure seemed like the devil took up the challenge.

Jack whipped around and locked eyes on Sam like a hawk on a hare. One of his signature wolfish grins spread across his chiseled face. "She wants another one, Rita, and I do too." Jack said something that made the guys at the bar laugh, then shook his friend's empty beer bottle at Rita as he set it on the bar.

Yep, time to go, Sam's gut yelled at her, and she started to slide to the end of the booth. She had only taken a step or two when Jack's presence pressed itself against her and a shot glass was shoved into her hand.

He made a *tsking* noise at her and shook his head slowly. "It ain't time to leave yet. I just got us drinks, sweetheart." He had moved in record time across the room, but now he talked as slow and sticky-sweet as molasses.

Allie headed to the bathroom, and Buster ambled over toward Sam's booth. "Well, where's mine, boss man?" Buster asked.

"Somewhere behind that bar, I reckon." Jack smiled offhandedly at him and then turned back to Sam. "Buster, I just got here, and Sam was about to go. Tell her she needs to stay just a bit longer. She's got a full drink left."

Buster looked from Jack to Sam to Jack again. His eyes reminded Sam of an eager dog confused at a command, not knowing if he should sit or roll over, but his smile never faded.

"Sam, sit down and stay awhile. I'm gonna get another, and I'll be right back. We can talk about some of the cars I've seen at the auction lot this week." He waved toward the booth and headed to the bar, leaving Sam looking up at Jack.

"Come on, just one drink, then you can go home to Grandma," Jack baited her.

"I already had one drink." She didn't rise to his barb, and her tone sounded bored in her own ears.

Her aloofness seemed to spark a glint in his eyes, and he moved one step closer. "Just one more, then. You'll have fun. You ain't had a real night on the town in Homestead yet, and I wanna be your welcome wagon."

Sam barked a laugh at that. "Tell me. How many times have you used that line, and how many times has it actually worked?"

He took one more step forward. "Just enough to lead me here to you."

Sam backed up one more step. Then her calves hit the booth, and she plopped down abruptly.

"Buckle up, honey. And scoot in." He leaned over to pull the shot glass directly in front of her before sliding into the other side of the booth with all the swagger of a panther, drunk on a new kill. He smelled like Old Spice with a little bit of sweat and grease underneath it all—the scent of a pure man, through and through. He kicked his cowboy boots up on the seat beside her, blocking her way out of the booth and grinning at her as he took another swig.

"Some would call this forced entrapment," she warned and took the first sip of the second shot she had sworn she wouldn't have.

"Some would call this love."

"I'm starting to think you are truly crazy."

"Only 'cause you're so pretty." He leaned on his elbows across the table and grinned at her boyishly.

She was beginning to understand why women flocked to him and believed his obviously bald-faced lies. He was a tad menacing one moment, then could be endearing in a sincere way two seconds later.

Before she could think about Jack any more, Buster and Allie joined them, and the conversation turned to Mustangs and mutts for what seemed like hours.

Jack kept the flirting to a minimum in mixed company, and Sam found it comforting to hang out with people her age in a party dynamic again. She hadn't realized how much she had isolated herself.

This is nice. I needed this, she told herself.

Jack ordered another beer, and one more shot for her. Was that the third one? Fourth?

"I need food," Sam finally stated.

"And I need to dance." Allie smiled at Buster.

He promptly took her hand and pulled her from the booth as "Sold (The Grundy County Auction Incident)" started up.

"Where's Rita Jo? I need some good greasy fries," Sam said, knowing that she needed carbs to balance out all the whiskey.

"She clocked out, and Viper took over." Jack nodded toward the balding man with a braided goatee and a tattoo sleeve, who was walking food out of the kitchen and to the bar. Jack whistled loudly, and Viper came right over to the booth.

"Alright. What can I get ya?" he asked.

"We wanna get two burger baskets and an extra order of fries."

"Do you have onion rings?" Sam asked.

"No, you don't need onion rings." Jack shook his head.

"On second thought, Mr. Viper, I want onions on my burger too. Double the onions please. Oh, and a large order of onion rings." Sam smiled sweetly and blinked at Jack. "You want anything else?"

Viper smiled, but Sam thought that if looks could kill, Jack would've buried her right there on the spot.

"Another beer," he grunted.

Viper walked back to the bar, and a man came up to the booth to talk about a car part he needed to order from Jack. They were visiting about carburetors when Sam realized that since Jack walked into the bar that night, she hadn't thought of Noah once.

This might not have been such a bad idea after all, the devil whispered, and Sam couldn't disagree. After the man shook Jack's hand

and left, Jack leaned back in his seat and eyed her. "You paying for dinner tonight?"

"For mine, obviously." Sam went to pull her wallet from her purse, and reality shattered her buzz. "Oh shit."

"What is it?"

"I left my wallet at the house."

Jack erupted in laughter. "Oh, I've heard this one before. Now tell me something, just how many times have you used that line, and how many times has it worked for you?"

"Shut up. I didn't mean to." She patted her leggings down though they had no pockets while her brain raced.

"This is quite a predicament. You better think quick because it's close to closing time, Sam. Ticktock, ticktock," he sang as he raised his beer bottle and swigged down the last of it.

"Buster will cover me, and I'll pay him back."

"Buster left a few minutes ago, honey. Allie wasn't feeling too spiffy, so they slipped out. Oh, Sam, I really hope you can wash dishes." Jack shook his head sarcastically.

Sam looked up and realized the bar had somehow almost completely emptied out while she talked to Jack, took time to use the restroom, and then ordered every onion on the menu just to spite him.

"How about I'll be a gentleman and buy you dinner tonight? I asked to do this back when we met, remember?"

Sam laughed at that. "Well, I guess you actually got your way after all, Mr. Reynolds."

"I always do."

Viper rang a big brass bell by the bar and declared it was last call to the few remaining stragglers. Then he walked over their burger baskets and tab to close. "Y'all got about fifteen minutes, and then the doors get locked."

"How much of the town have you truly got to explore?" Jack asked as they ate their food.

"Not much outside of Kathleen's places and the bookstore." She didn't want to say Noah's name.

"Well, that's nothing. I got something I wanna show you. I think you'd like it."

"Sounds like fun!" She pasted on a wide, fake smile. "Are we meeting Kara there?"

His cheek twitched a bit. "No, me and her ain't a thing anymore."

"She was in the bookstore the other day, and she seemed so sweet. I don't get why you'd want to run around on her. That's really messed up," Drunk Sam said through a mouthful of onion ring.

"Who said I cheated on her?" His tone was edgy.

"Umm, like, the whole town? You don't hide it." Sam swung an onion ring wide for emphasis.

Jack grinned wryly and then sobered, averting his eyes to the table in front of him. "I haven't been the best to her, I know. She deserves better than I can give her. I tried, Sam, I really did. I wanted to be what she needed, and it'd work for a little while. But then I'd find myself wanting more. I didn't feel that spark with her that I know is out there. It's like my body knew deep down she's not my person. It was painful to finally accept it. And I hurt her for longer than I should have by not accepting it before now."

Okay, ouch. Sam bit the inside of her cheek as Chase came to mind. And the hundreds of small things Sam tried to be, the things that she thought Chase wanted of her had only mocked her. The Lilly Pulitzer dresses she wore because his mother loved them even though Sam hated them. Straightening her naturally wavy hair every morning because Chase liked it that way. And all the other things that the mirror couldn't detect.

A thousand little paper cuts were needed to trim her down into the shape and size Chase had wanted, and it still wasn't enough. Years of passive-aggressive ways to get his point across had shredded the person that was Samantha into nothing but what he wanted. The memories themselves like asbestos into Sam's softest spots, and over time carved her out as a new person. She was made in God's likeness but had molded herself for a man's liking.

"Ground Control to Major Sam." Jack snapped his fingers in front of her as he pushed his empty basket to the end of the booth. "You still in there?"

"Yeah, sorry. I had a lot on my mind today. It's past my bedtime anyway. Your story got me thinking about my past, and I zoned out."

Jack leaned forward now and covered her hand with his and squeezed it. "Hmm, well I'm here whenever you wanna unload. We could find a quiet place to talk."

The warm roughness of his hand felt good on Sam's knuckles, but suddenly she felt the overpowering need to get out of there. She refused to let herself fall for Jack's charm. There were already enough notches on his bedpost without her adding to it.

"Maybe another day." She pulled her hand back and started to stand up. "I gotta head back to Rose Garden now. Thanks for din-ner. I promise I'll pay you back."

"You ain't paying me back. Besides, I'm walking you home," he said, getting out of his booth.

"I'm fine on my own, Jack."

"No you aren't. You ain't got that mutt of yours, so somebody's gotta make sure you get home alright." He waved to Viper as he opened the door for her.

The moon was full and brilliant. The dirt road glowed like a silver snake winding through the trees up ahead. Jack reached out and grabbed her hand and told her to mind the step when the sidewalk ended. He didn't let go as they started into the wooded section of the path, and she let him hold it.

Isn't this what I wanted with someone? she asked herself.

Someone to hold the door for her, to put her hand in his, to walk her home, and to make her laugh. Her past was aching proof that she had been known to misjudge character. Maybe she had been all wrong about Jack Reynolds as well as Noah. A pang ran through her when she thought of him. At that exact moment, Jack squeezed her hand silently—like somehow he knew.

"I wanna show you something." Jack tugged at her hand, but she pulled back.

"Another night. I wanna get home."

"Fine." His tone told her that he didn't like her answer, but he didn't argue. "Go to the back door. Kathleen has a key behind the red flowerpot near the swing. The floors are less creaky in the kitchen anyhow. It's easier to slip in that way," he said and led the way around the house.

"How do you know all this?" Sam asked.

"My great-uncle Thurman was married to Kathleen. I used to spend the summers with them." He shrugged and flashed a smile toward her.

As they were about to round the corner of the house, Jack pushed Sam back against the clapboard siding and kissed her.

She wasn't expecting it and nearly gagged when he forced his tongue into her mouth. The clapboard siding hurt her back. She tried to step forward, but his hand cupped her face roughly, and his mouth locked on hers again while his arm held her steady against his chest. She didn't know if it was Jack Reynolds or Jack Daniels, but something made her kiss him back. They made out like high schoolers, his hands raking down her body and pulling her closer, while her hands tugged at his hair in the spotlight the moon provided.

He was a good kisser, but when his fingers brushed the top of her yoga pants and touched skin, her whole body rebelled. She pulled back and promptly puked down the side of the house and onto Jack's Lucchese boots.

He cursed and jumped away.

Oh God, Sam moaned, not knowing if she just thought the words or if she said them aloud. She held herself up with one hand on the house. Her other hand tried to keep her hair back the best she could.

She wondered where Jack had gone, and then she saw him walk back around the side of the house with a water hose in his hand that was already sputtering water. He sprayed his boots and then the house, washing her embarrassment down into the rose bushes lining the wall.

Jack had evidently had enough of her at that point. "Well, darlin', it's time you got some sleep. Didn't know you had a weak stomach."

"Yeah." Sam couldn't say more.

She was mortified, but more than that, she clenched her teeth and kept swallowing to keep from throwing up again. She didn't remember getting to her room or the bathroom, but she did remember throwing up again and brushing her teeth before crawling into bed. She had fitful dreams and woke up with a blistering hangover, the likes of which she couldn't compare with anything she'd suffered in the past.

She slowly dragged her wretched body downstairs after dry heaving by the door and was immensely relieved they didn't have any guests at that time. The smell of greasy bacon or scrambled eggs would send her into a sick tailspin for sure.

Kathleen grinned when Sam made it down to the kitchen, and she poured coffee into her mug. "Look what the cat drug in this morning! How's that head of yours feeling, honey?"

Sam would've rolled her eyes if she didn't think that would make her barf again. "If you could keep your berating to a whisper today, I'd greatly appreciate it."

"Poor thing." Kathleen chuckled. "I got a fix that'll get you back on your feet. Loretta and I were just sitting in the garden since it's a pretty day. You go out there, and I'll bring you some coffee and toast and a quick fix of our own making to get you back right. And then I want to hear all about last night."

Sam almost groaned but instead made her way outside, following a plume of smoke to where Loretta sat on a white wrought iron lounge that matched the tea table and chairs. She was chewing on a cigar, staring past the roses and the barricade they had built around this sitting area and scanning the tree line, lost in thought. The fact that the roses created a sort of privacy fence made Sam think of *The Secret Garden*, a book she had read as a child.

"How do you feel?" Loretta smiled around her cigar, squinting through the smoke at Sam once she realized she was approaching.

"Exactly how you'd think I'd feel, smarty-pants." Sam groaned as she sat down as far away from Loretta's cigar as possible to keep from going back into a fit of nausea.

In a few minutes, Kathleen joined them with a little wooden tray full of Sam's saving grace. Coffee with a splash of cream, white toast with strawberry jam, and a mixture that looked like a potion that she would mix up in the yard as a child.

"Drink that first, it'll help the most."

"Do I have to?" Sam winced at the smell.

"Yes!" the old women answered in unison.

Sam held her nose and shot it down. It tasted as bad as it smelled, and Sam's whole body shook as she swallowed the last of it. She quickly followed it with big mouthfuls of hot coffee.

"What in the hell was in that?" she sputtered through a gag.

"Everything good that these woods have to offer. You know, the more I work with nature, the more firmly I believe God didn't forget a thing when He made this earth. All the cures for everything that ails us can be found if we look close enough."

"Amen," Loretta puffed out.

"Oh, Rita Jo called this morning—she said you need to be on the lookout for Kara. She may seek you out for a good old catfight because you left the bar last night with Jack," Kathleen said as she took a sip of her coffee and leaned back into her chair.

Sam's face reddened. "Do people literally have nothing else to talk about in this town?"

"Nope." Loretta puffed out her second ring of smoke with her answer.

"Sam, I know we've warned you about Jack before, but I feel the need to warn you again," Kathleen said seriously. "I know that you're a grown woman and you've proven that you can take care of yourself, but Jack's got demons he's fighting. There's a curse on men in the Reynolds bloodline, and there's a mean streak through all of 'em. My Thurman was pretty like Jack, and he couldn't keep his belt buckled either." She spread butter on a second piece of toast and passed it to Sam. "It's going to take a woman willing to put the fear of God into Jack to ever make him settle down, and I don't know if that would even work. I tried with Thurman, but nothing stopped him from doing what he wanted. He cheated on me when we were just starting to date and too many times to count after we were married."

"Why did you marry him, then?"

"Because I was told to. I thought my daddy was God when I was a girl. Whatever he said was law. I didn't know about Thurman's running around at the time. I only found out once he got sloppy with his alibis. I didn't know that I had any other options than staying with him. Besides, I had my boys to look after," Kathleen's answered.

She stared out at the tree line just visible above the rambling roses, her eyes setting in the same space Loretta seemed to gaze at earlier. "I was in the hospital in labor with Bubba when I found out Thurman was sleeping with that rat-faced Tammy Cox. I'd hired her to keep Andrew while I was in the hospital on bed rest near the end of carrying Bubba, and Thurman was already running round with her right under my nose then. I moved all my stuff to a spare bedroom when I came home after delivery. I ripped some of my stitches doing it too, but I didn't give a damn. I couldn't share a bed with him anymore. He demanded a divorce that day, but I wouldn't give it to him."

"Why?" Sam was intrigued, watching Kathleen clench her jaw slightly and tighten her eyes on the woods beyond the yard.

"This house was built by my ancestors when this area was tobacco and cotton country instead of piney woods. It passed down from mother to daughter until it reached me. If I had divorced him, I would've had to sell it and give him half or else buy him out. I didn't have enough money to do that, so I turned the place into a bed-and-breakfast and made sure that the lawyer fixed things so that Thurman couldn't get his greedy little hands on a dime of my money. We lived together until the boys were grown and gone," she explained, "and then he died."

"Was it cancer or something else?" Sam asked.

"Nope, he just went to sleep and never woke up. The old doctor we had in those days said it was probably a heart attack," Kathleen replied.

"Did your sons know? About him cheating on you?"

"Not 'til their teenage years. By then, Thurman was about as good at hiding his running around as Jack is. Both of my boys blamed me too. They thought their daddy did no wrong. Besides, they couldn't judge him for that. It would just be the pots calling the kettle black. Andrew's on his fourth wife now, and Bubba has been divorced twice already. All their ex-wives filed on charges of adultery," Kathleen answered. "I'm telling you to be careful with Jack. There's something that taints a bloodline. I don't know what it is or what caused it. All I know is I've never met a woman who could break it."

Sam had a million more questions but read the energy surrounding her and held her tongue. She had known Jack was a rake from the moment she laid eyes on him, and she needed to heed their warning when it came to Jack—she knew that instinctively.

"What led you to the bar last night anyways?" Loretta looked over and tapped her cigar over the crystal ashtray.

Sam told them everything.

"Seems to me like we'll need to have another little prayer session soon," Loretta said. "We need to get to church too. Sam, honey, come with us this Sunday. It'll do us all good. You'll also get to meet a little more of the community. There's more men than Jack and Noah in Texas. You need to remember that."

Sam just nodded, the lump in her throat slowly dissolving the more coffee she drank and the longer the three women sat in the garden, trying to solve all the problems of the world.

CHAPTER SEVEN

THE POT AND THE KETTLE

PART TWO

Noah had been taught what was right and what was wrong since birth. An integral part of his being was centered on behaving how his parents and grandfather would have wanted him to act. And he thought that he would have made them proud if they were still alive. As a child he used to pray that heaven had a mezzanine, so his parents could look down and see him. At thirty-six, he still prayed that was true.

He had done what he had set out to do. He had a successful business, earning respect in his hometown on his own merits, not on his family name or influence. He'd even reallocated the Carter home and made it into a school, something his mother had always dreamed of doing. His grandfather had wanted a bookstore, and he had completed that dream too.

When Sam had walked into his life, he was standing right on the edge of proposing to Laura. His plan to buy a ring before the end of summer now had him hesitating. He thought they would get engaged, start planning the wedding and house they wanted to build. Settle down. Grow old together—as long as Laura said that they could grow old in Homestead. Back years ago, when they had first started getting serious, she had agreed, but these days she had set her heels against the idea.

He hated himself for dreaming about Sam. He would have avoided it if he could control it, but she invaded his sleep. He'd wake up swearing that he could smell her perfume in his bedroom. He was still scolding himself when the store phone rang. In his rush, he knocked a stack of books on the floor on his way across the room.

"Hello!" he said breathlessly.

"What were you doing to be so out of breath?" Laura asked.

Laura never called on the landline, so he had thought the call might be coming from Sam. He eased down in the chair behind his desk, and a thick fog of guilt settled on his shoulders like a wet blanket on a boulder.

"I can't even get a *Hey there* or *How was your day?*" His tone sounded flat in his own ears.

"I called your cell phone five times, and you didn't pick up. I've told you to keep it in your pocket and turned on," Laura snapped, her voice colored with the tones of deep-rooted anger. "We have to talk. Today. I left work half an hour early. I am calling to tell you that I'm coming your way. You'll need to close the shop up early."

"What's going on now, Laura?" Noah bit back a sigh. "After that scene you made at the community meeting, the whole town's been asking if you've moved back to Homestead so you can run for mayor."

"What do you think, Noah? Are you going to move to Jefferson or stay there in our parents' shadows and grow mold?" she fired back. "I thought you might just move on and grow up once you got done grieving. But now I think you're staying there to rot just to be near your new little red-haired friend."

Noah shivered at her cold tone. "I'm not leaving Homestead, and that decision was made long before Sam ever came to town. Let's not argue over the phone. How far are you out?"

"Not far enough," she grumbled and ended the call.

Noah laid the receiver on the desk and strode back to the pile of books he had knocked over earlier and launched a copy of *Moby Dick* clear across the room with a strong kick.

Childish, he scolded himself.

Yes, he was tired of this, but grown men didn't throw books.

This wasn't the first time that Laura had wanted to *talk*. It was a term she held over his head like a threat, always centering on the same old list of things he must do—sell the bookstore, move to Jefferson, buy a big house and do something with his life, anything more exciting or impressive than owning a bookshop.

He didn't want to hash all that out over again. Not today. Not ever again. He had burned his bridge with Sam so that Laura would never need to feel jealous. Nothing had ever happened other than that one time when they came close to sharing a kiss. But he had known he couldn't because it'd hurt Laura and Sam both.

When the bell above the door rang, Noah was picking up the abused books. Laura flipped the sign in the door to say closed, switched the deadbolt, and turned back to him, raising a paper bag in front of her in a sign of peace. "I stopped and got some cornbread sandwiches from that little café that you like. Let's take them to the back where we can be comfortable." Her tone had changed back to the one he knew from two years ago—sweet, kind, and soft.

She sat down in Nibbler's usual chair and put the brown paper bag on the small table between them. "First of all, I need to apologize to you, Noah. I'm sorry for arguing so much lately. I just can't stand the thought of you wasting your life here. You have so much potential. I just feel like as your friend, I need to push you—" She caught herself and stopped short, but her voice was still soft and almost sorrowful.

"What? As my girlfriend? Or just as my friend? Or is it now as an acquaintance?" Noah asked in a measured tone. "Well, go on, I'd like to hear what you have to say."

She opened her mouth and snapped it shut again. She opened the sack and laid the sandwiches out on paper napkins. "As your friend," she repeated slowly, "in my opinion, you will always be the nerd that you were in high school if you stay in this place your whole life."

"Laura, it is difficult, but at some point, you've got to let high school go. I don't know what to tell you. I didn't care what people thought of me then, and I don't care what they think of me now. What if you didn't care either?" he asked.

"You should, and I do . . . or did . . . Whatever!" She threw up her hands and looked at Noah with desperation. "How do you really feel about me, Noah? Down, down in your heart, and be honest."

"Well, that just came out of nowhere," he said, standing up, too restless to sit. "Where is this stemming from?"

"Look, in the past few months, we have had supper together once a week when you were willing to drive down to my apartment in Jefferson and open the shop later the next morning. Or I've dropped in when I have some courthouse business here in Homestead, and that's it. It's been almost five months since we had sex, Noah—something's wrong between us. I feel it, and I know you feel it too. We've drifted apart so much that I feel like I barely know you," she said.

"You can't blame all of our problems on me wanting to stay in Homestead."

"I know." She sighed. "It's an impasse that we both don't want to give on. You still didn't answer my question."

"Which one?" Noah asked.

"How do you feel about me?"

"Is this all about the rumors going around about me and Sam? Nothing has happened. She and I are friends, and that's all. It was nice to have someone to talk books with."

"Rita Jo told me that she could see sparks between you two," she answered.

"You know me better than that. Have I ever, one time, cheated on you?"

"No, but . . ." Her eyes filled with tears.

He sat down and turned to focus on her. "What are you trying to say, Laura?"

"I want to know if you love me," she answered, her voice getting shakier, "or if you're just with me?"

"I love you, Laura," Noah said.

"Why?"

"You were there for me when I lost my grandfather."

"That's a crappy reason. Do I make your heart flutter when you hear my voice? When you kiss me, do your knees buckle? Am I the first thing you think about in the morning, and the last at night before you go to sleep?" she asked.

"Why are you asking me all this now?" Noah couldn't honestly answer the questions without upsetting her.

"You are not *in love* with me, are you?" Laura asked, standing up and setting her chin, her fists balled up and at her sides. "You aren't, and I know it. I hate hydrangeas. You sent flowers to my work, and it was practically a whole bouquet of white hydrangeas. They make me think of my grandma's funeral. I told you that back when we used to sneak onto Miller's farmland to go swimming in the pond out back, but you didn't remember. And you remember everything you ever read, but you didn't remember that?"

Noah rolled his eyes, and she held up a palm. "Let me finish. You don't look at me like you used to. I ignored it at first. I thought I loved you . . . I mean, I do love you, I want only the best for you. But . . ." She shook her head and freed the tears to flow down her cheeks. "I'm not *in love* with you. I'm sorry, Noah."

Noah's first emotion was a crashing wave of relief. The second was immense guilt for that being his initial reaction. The third emotion was a healthy pairing of anger and confusion.

"You've been accusing me of cheating on you since Sam moved to town, but the whole while you knew you didn't love me or want to be with me? Why didn't you just tell me before and finish this?"

"I didn't know for sure," she blurted, "but then I figured out I was right. I love you as a friend, as a confidant, but nothing more. I understand the difference now." The silence that followed was deafening.

Now? Noah's blood roared.

"How long?"

Those two words made Laura put her face in her hands and start to cry. "Since Christmas." She hiccupped behind her fingers.

Noah stood and walked a few feet away. He stared at the opposite wall, not daring to look at her. "Does he live here?"

"No, in Jefferson. At least for a little while longer." She sniffed. "I never meant to hurt you, Noah. I didn't mean for it to happen. I went to that Christmas party by myself, and he was there too, and he helped me get home. It was completely innocent at first . . ." she stammered and repeated, "I never meant for it to happen."

"He's a coworker, then?"

"Of sorts." Her answer was short.

He prodded her. "Of sorts?"

"He got hired last summer to do maintenance work at the courthouse and Jefferson's government buildings. My office is connected directly to the utility closet—he's a good man, extremely creative and hardworking, and it just happened." Laura had pulled her hands from her reddened face. "He's moving around doing odd jobs for a year 'til he settles down. He's a surfer, and he's leaving soon . . ." She hesitated and then added, "He wants me to go with him."

A truck could've run Noah over at that moment, and he wouldn't have noticed. He was dumbstruck. How did he not see this coming? She had been distant and argumentative over the past half year, sure, but he didn't have a clue as to when their dynamic had changed.

"So now instead of aiming for a mansion and being mayor of Homestead, you're going to live the van life and surf every day?"

Laura laughed. "I love him, Noah. I know it sounds crazy because it does to me. It's nothing like I thought I wanted, but I do want it. I love him. And he's crazy about me."

This declaration knocked the wind out of him for a moment. Finally, he asked, "What's the lucky guy's name?"

"Declan." Laura gave him a watery smile and wiped more black mascara tears from her cheeks. "He inherited his uncle's old surf shop in Hawaii last month, and he's itching to get to work on it. My last day at the courthouse is Friday. We fly out Saturday morning."

"Why did you even come to that last meeting at the B&B? You had to have already given your notice, right?" Noah asked, sitting back down across from her and motioning for her to do the same.

"Appearances, and then I just got triggered," she answered with another shrug. "Rita Jo and Kara are the nosiest people in town. They were determined that you'd propose and I'd move back here, and they started getting suspicious when I stopped visiting so much. Rumors are the bread and butter in small towns, so I had to be careful until Declan and I figured out how we truly felt about each other before dropping this nuke of a talking point for the town to sink its teeth in."

"Did you tell your mama?" Noah asked. "She deserves to know that you are leaving Texas."

"I'm going up there when I leave here." She sighed. "She's going to think I'm crazy, but that's the way she's always seen me."

"I know y'all have your differences, but she really loves you. You're all she's got."

"I know." Laura sniffed. "I promise I'm gonna tell her. I'll call too, and maybe she will come visit me."

"I think she'd like that. Alright, let's sit down and eat these sandwiches you brought." Noah changed the subject.

He and Laura were over. She was in love with someone else, and Noah was free to think about anyone he wanted. His mind raced, and he tried his best to tamper it down.

"You know I won't ever forget you showing up to the house the day after Granddaddy died. You had your hair pulled back with a little blue ribbon. And you had spilled some of the crockpot of chili you were carrying on the front of your shirt. You could've spit fire, but I always thought you were the prettiest girl in town, even with half a crockpot of chili on your shirt." Noah smiled at the memory.

Laura stopped mid-bite and looked up at Noah. "I thought you were such a nerd."

"Well, you weren't wrong. If your mama hadn't sent you up there with food for me, I don't know if you would've ever given me the time of day."

"You grew on me," Laura said. "You were kind and goofy. And you had a butler. The younger me fell for you real quick."

"I want this to end on good terms. I want us to still be friends. I don't want to lose you as a friend."

Laura laid her other hand on top of his. "You aren't losing anything, Noah. You'll always be my friend."

"Remember helping me freeze all the casseroles and stack them in that tiny little freezer after the funeral?" he asked. "That was the beginning of our friendship."

"I'm sure there's probably still some green bean casserole ice cubes wedged in the back even today."

"You may be right." Noah's heart was lighter than it had been in years.

He hadn't lost Laura as a friend. He had gained something in this moment of truth. It seemed like a weight had been lifted from her as well. "That meant the world to me, Laura. How you helped me navigate through all of that—the funeral stuff you figured out, and all the smallest details you helped me work through. I hate we are ending quite this way, but I appreciate what we've had."

"Me too." Laura looked like she was about to cry again. "There was a time in our relationship where part of the reason I was with you was because of your inheritance. I know that's bad to say, but I needed to tell you. Something in me told me I could set everything right if we got married back then. I thought it'd make me happy. I just didn't want to be a Henton anymore in this damn town."

"You don't have to explain. I get it. All is forgiven." Noah stood again and held out his hand.

Laura looked at him, confused. "What?"

"Let's dance."

Laura stared up at Noah. "Are you serious?"

"The first time I ever brought you into the bookshop, we danced to something playing on that little black camping radio Granddaddy had. I want us to dance to it one last time, as friends."

"If we weren't breaking up, I would almost think this was romantic." Laura smiled as she took Noah's hand and stood.

"Declan has nothing to worry about," Noah said as he switched on the radio when they walked past and then pulled her into his arms. A Randy Travis song came through the static.

"Did you stay with me just because of my inheritance? You can be honest now."

"That wasn't all of it. I was pissed when you gave the Carter house up for a school to move into, sure. But the house and the cars weren't all of it. You made me believe in myself. You saw me how I wanted to see myself."

"I saw you as the girl with the blue ribbon in her hair, who walked a mile and a half to bring chili to me. I still sometimes see you like that. That's when I fell for you."

"When did you fall out of love with me?" Her question stilled his heart for a moment.

When did I stop caring for Laura in that way?

"I don't really know, Laura. I'm sorry, but I can't really pinpoint it."

"That's okay." She sighed and rested her head on his chest as they swayed, his hand rubbing small comforting circles on her upper back.

They danced in silence for a bit before talking again, holding each other and letting their bodies say their farewells with the last embrace.

"Thank you for this," Laura finally said against the front of his shirt.

"For what?" Noah asked as he looked down at the top of her head.

"For not screaming at me and going berserk. I have dreaded telling you for weeks now."

"The worrying was punishment enough, then, for you not telling me sooner. I've only had friendly breakups, and I intend to keep it that way. I know that some of us aren't so lucky."

"Don't even say his name," Laura warned.

"I didn't," Noah stated simply.

Laura held on to Noah even tighter. "I swear he stalks me sometimes. Anytime I'm in Homestead, I can feel his eyes on me."

"Jack Reynolds knows not to mess with you since the day that you put him in his place. And the sheriff backed you up on it."

"I know, I just don't trust him as far as I can throw him."

"Well, you won't have to worry about him soon enough. You better remember to pack sunscreen, a whole suitcase of it. You'll fry out there in that island sun."

Laura threw back her head and giggled. "That's what Declan said."

A flicker of movement flashed in the window, and Noah could've sworn he saw Sam's face through the glass, but when he blinked, she was gone. Laura said something Noah didn't quite catch, and he shook his head and looked back at her face. "You're a million miles away right now, Noah."

"Sorry."

"It's the redhead, ain't it? Do you like her?"

"She hasn't done anything wrong, so please don't bring her into our mess."

"I had hoped you liked her, so it would soften the blow when I told you. Or make me look a little less like a villain in the situation." Laura seemed to study him when he didn't answer, and then went on. "I hope you find your person, Noah, whether it's her or some other woman. I really want you to be happy—as happy as I am."

Laura leaned up and kissed him on the cheek before stepping away to grab her purse and coat from the back room. "I'll come by tomorrow morning to get my stuff from your place if that's alright. I'm gonna stay with Mama tonight."

"She'd like that," Noah agreed and walked her to the door.

"Thank you again, Noah, I'm sorry how this all turned out."

"Love makes one want to do crazy things. There's no need to apologize anymore. Tell your mama hello for me. I'll see you tomorrow."

Noah stood at the front door after Laura left for what seemed like minutes, just staring through the glass and into the distance. In a matter of hours, plans for his whole life had changed.

He should call Sam. No, he shouldn't. He was torn between wanting to talk to her and feeling like he should wait till Laura told everyone she wanted to and had left town before he talked to Sam.

He walked back to the reading area and eased down into Sam's chair and chuckled. Laura had sat in Nibbler's chair the whole time they talked and had not sniffled or sneezed one time. Thinking of Nibbler brought Sam back in his mind, and he wondered what she was doing at that very moment. He could've sworn he saw her in the window, but it must've been his imagination.

His thoughts were a jumbled mess, going from his grandfather to Laura and then Sam and the way she had looked at him when he had caught her that day when she tripped. After a while, he stood back up and started his end-of-day routine of switching everything off for the night. As he finished in the back and started across the front room, a memory popped into his mind. He saw Samantha standing there, wrestling with all her baggage and her dog straining his leash to get a whiff of Noah. She looked both helpless and determined somehow. He remembered wanting to strangle Jack Reynolds that night, but looking back now, he was grateful Jack had been an ass and made her walk.

Since he lived right next door to Justine in the same trailer park, staying on the futon downstairs would be his best move. It would give Laura and Justine a bit more privacy tonight, and he'd be distracted driving anyway. He was about to open the door to go to the speakeasy when the landline rang.

It was one of his vendors from the Dallas area, and he sounded excited. "I bought out the last remnants of a secondhand bookstore that had to close its doors. I've got a box with about fifty historical romances and at least thirty moderns. Are you interested? They are all in pristine condition. If you are, I can ship them to you on Monday."

"Yes, definitely. What else did you get?" Noah asked.

"There's about a hundred cowboy romances, mostly from bestselling authors," he answered.

"If there's a cowboy on the cover, it will sell in Texas, so I'll take them too," Noah said. Maybe Sam would agree to write reviews on cowboys as well as her normal historical romances. It seemed like everything turned his thoughts toward her and he couldn't do a thing about it.

When the call ended, Noah had to talk himself out of calling the Rose Garden or just swinging by. It was too late for either one. He'd scare the old ladies to death at that hour. He realized he had never gotten Sam's cell phone number, but maybe that was a good thing. He lay down on the futon downstairs and stared at the floor joists above him, wondering what Sam was doing at that exact moment, and he thought about exactly how and what he would say when he told her about what had happened that evening.

When he had changed the store times, he had called Kathleen instead of being truthful to Sam. It was taking the coward's way out, trying to please Laura without directly hurting Sam. Now that Laura was out of his life, he was going to do this right if given the chance to, and so he lay there on his back until he fell asleep with Sam still on his mind.

Noah searched Rose Garden as he drove past, and didn't see hide nor hair of any of its inhabitants, and in a few minutes, he pulled up to his trailer just as Laura came out of her mother's trailer. She wore Justine's terry cloth robe wrapped tightly against the morning chill. The two of them worked in silence as they gathered what few belongings Laura had left over the years at Noah's place. She had brought in his stuff and set it on the sofa. Two minutes after she left, a soft knock rapped at the door. Laura's mother, Justine, stood on his doorstep with a plate of cookies in her hands and a mournful look on her face.

"I had to bring these over. Oh, Noah, I am so sorry," she said with a trembling chin.

Noah stood to the side and motioned her inside. "Come on in. Are those peanut butter?"

Justine nodded. "Yes, they are. I know they are your favorite . . ." She wiped at her eyes with the tail of her apron and stood in the middle of Noah's living room like a guilty man in court for his judgment day. "Laura told me everything last night. I could barely sleep. My baby is finally leaving me. I knew deep down this day was coming, and then she did you wrong, Lord, after all you've been through—" Justine squeezed her eyes shut and shook her head. "The only consolation is that she seems happy, and there's a part of me that is so relieved to see my baby finally happy, but I just . . ." she stammered, "I hate how this all happened. You are a good man, Noah Carter, you deserve the world, and you are worthy of so much better than to be treated a fool."

"It's alright, Justine. All's well that ends well. You really have nothing to apologize for. We ended up on a good note after all. I was just about to make a pot of coffee. Let me get it going, and we can have cookies with our coffee," he assured her on his way to the kitchen. "Laura's and my relationship died in its sleep years ago. I think it actually came as a relief to both of us to know we felt the same way about it. I'm not hurting, so neither of you have anything to be sorry for, I promise."

Justine set the cookies on the narrow coffee table and eased down on the end of the sofa as the coffeepot started spitting. "Are you sure?"

"I'm positive. I'm glad that she valued our friendship enough to be honest with me before she left." Noah didn't care to talk any more about Laura. He had woken up that morning ready to let it all go. "Now tell me, did you finish those last books you got at the store?"

"Not quite yet," she answered and pulled a couple of tissues from her pocket that she must've squirreled away before walking over. "I've been putting my feet up after my shift at the grocery store every evening, and binge-watching *Justified*."

"James Lee Burke for reading and Raylan Givens for watching. You have good taste." Noah chuckled as he pulled two mugs down from the cabinet above the toaster.

"I'm a woman who knows what she likes." Justine laughed. "You are not pretending to be fine to make me feel better, are you? That would be so like you."

He filled one mug and then the next from the coffeepot as it was still brewing, the dripping coffee sizzling as he handed one to her on the couch and went back for his. "No, ma'am, I am not pretending. Laura and I ended things the best we could, so there's no hard feelings. It's alright, Ms. Henton."

"Don't call me that. I'm just Justine." She blew on the top of the mug and took a sip as Noah laughed. "I'm glad you are a good enough man to not react harshly. Lord have mercy! I remember her coming home covered in bruises after breaking things off with Jack. I still blame that boy for making her go against me for so long. I tried to come between them when she went back, and that was the first time she told me that she never wanted to see me again."

Laura had never told Noah about the bruises, or anything about Jack being physically violent with her. Noah knew Jack had a temper. The whole town knew that, but this was sickening news to him. In his thoughts Sam flickered past the anger, but he swore if Jack touched Sam, he would bury the man.

"Laura never told me how Jack treated her. I would've beat down his door if I had known." Noah wondered what else Laura had hidden. "Did y'all have a good chat last night?"

"She apologized for all the times when she was downright bitchy to me. And promised to call me every single Sunday afternoon. And she's happy and in love with this surfer boy," Justine answered. "I feel like old prayers I had forgotten I had prayed have finally been answered."

"Maybe you can fly to Hawaii next Christmas," Noah suggested.

"Laura suggested that too, but I've never been on a plane. I might do something stupid."

Noah finished off his first cookie and picked up a second one. "You'd be fine. Anyone able to cook like you is smart enough to figure out an airport. What season of *Justified* are you watching?"

"Just about to start season two," she answered.

"That's a good one," Noah said. "What time do you go in today?"

"I go in at three p.m. for the early dinner shift."

"Let's watch an episode, I'm not opening the store till noon. I could use some time off."

"I would like that very much, Noah." The older woman smiled warmly. "Like I said, you are a good man."

"And you, Justine, are a good person and a great mother. You aren't losing me in this breakup either," he said and saw her eyes prick with tears again. They watched in silence side by side on the couch and drank the whole pot of coffee by the end of the second episode.

CHAPTER EIGHT

NO, I AIN'T

Noah's first thought upon waking up the next morning was Sam. He got to the store in record time even though he let his truck crawl at a snail's pace when he was passing by Kathleen's. Though he was determined to be patient and wait a few days, he couldn't stop himself from picking up the phone more than a dozen times in the next two days. But he never took it past the dial tone.

The way that gossip spread through Homestead, she had to have heard about Laura breaking up with him because the town seemed to be choking on the news. Some acted as if there had been a death in the community instead of an ordinary breakup. Folks that Noah grew up with bowed their heads in public and talked quietly when they saw him. The day after Laura started telling folks that she and Noah had broken up, a gaggle of older ladies started bringing casseroles and cakes, quickly turning the bookshop into a funeral wake with their hushed murmurs and nine-by-thirteen casseroles all in a row on his desk.

"I just gotta be patient," he said to the black landline receiver hanging closest to the brownies. "She deserves time to process, and when Kathleen sends her down for another round of books, I'll be ready."

He was resolute for most of the two days. By morning three though, Noah was biting at the bit. He picked up the phone to call Kathleen and let her know he'd be open until seven again. His hand was holding the phone receiver when the bell above the door chimed and startled him. He swung around to find Rita Jo with an armful of doughnuts, and his hopes instantly deflated. He had thought and wished just for a moment that Sam had finally shown up.

"Hey, darlin'," Rita Jo said as she crossed the floor in a sexy strut. "I brought you something to ease your pain. Sweets always help me when I'm down and blue. I thought a taste of doughnuts could help distract you from your heartache." She rounded the end of the desk, sat down in his lap without ceremony, and hugged him tightly until he awkwardly hugged her back.

"Thank you for your sympathy and the doughnuts, but Laura and I broke up on friendly terms. What we had was over a long time ago, and we both admitted it. We're fine with moving on as friends. I don't want to drop you on the floor, but I really need to stand up and shelve some books."

"Well, then." Rita Jo stood up and took both his hands in hers. "You're convincing, but I don't buy it. You're the kinda man that will hide his pain inside, but honey, I'm here for you for whatever you need." She gave him a sly wink and batted her lashes. "And I do mean whatever. How about we go for a drink when you get off work this evening?"

"Thank you." Noah smiled and said, "but I have plans already."

Rita Jo straightened up and eyed him carefully. "With the redhead? She's the real reason that you and Laura broke up, isn't she? Everyone in Homestead knows that y'all have been carrying on."

Noah sucked in a lungful of air and let it out slowly. "You shouldn't believe everything you hear, Rita Jo."

Rita Jo picked up the box of doughnuts again and swung back to look at Noah, her mouth in a tight line now instead of a sweet smile. "If you aren't grieving and needing someone to lean on, I'll take these back. Seems you're getting enough sympathy elsewhere." She marched out of the bookstore without even looking back, leaving Noah wondering where the hell that had come from.

It was only a few hours after Rita had left when Noah finally caved and picked up the landline. He punched in the phone number to the B&B and was preparing to leave a message when Kathleen's voice cut off the fifth ring. "Hello, Noah. How are you doing, my boy?"

"I'm doing just fine. I hope you're doing good too. I—uh—I'm sure the gossip train has already gotten up the hill by now. Don't know what you've heard, but I wanted to assure you that all is well. Laura is happy, and I'm happy for her. All's well that ends well." He heard himself using that line too much. He stopped and cleared his throat when Kathleen didn't respond. "I just wanted to see how y'all were doing and let you know that I'm going back to my later hours at the shop now."

"Well, that's good to hear. Just know we all love ya and we'll be praying for you through all this. And Laura too, I hope she found happiness as you said. Her mama deserves to know her baby is going to be okay." Kathleen's tone was a tad diplomatic and reserved in comparison to how she normally spoke.

"I agree with that. I have talked to Justine, and she is taking it pretty well. And I'm fine. Really, Kathleen, I mean it. I am not in pain. My heart is not broken," he declared.

"If you are being honest with me and yourself, then I'm glad for you. You deserve to find your own happiness too, honey." She spoke to someone in the background before returning. "The little lady I hired to clean the rooms just got here. I should go."

"Sure, Kathleen, but would you give Sam my cell phone number and tell her to call me? Please? I haven't seen her in a long while now," Noah said. "I would love to talk to her, just to hear her voice."

She hesitated for a few seconds before she said, "Noah, she hasn't been feeling too good and been mighty busy with other things. She may need a little time."

"Yeah, totally." Noah stammered a bit. "Anything I can do to help?"

"Prayers and patience do wonders, so just pray and be patient, okay?" Her tone sounded cheery even as she lowered to a whisper. "Healing is a slow process."

"I can do that. Tell her I called, please, and if any of you need a fresh round of books, just let me know. I can run them by any evening on my way home."

"Will do," Kathleen said. "Bye now."

That was completely unlike the Kathleen he had known all of his life. He normally couldn't get a word in edgewise when he called her. He wondered what Sam was sick with—or sick from. If Kathleen said to give her time, he would do that. But what exactly would she need time to heal from? Other than her heartbreak in her hometown. Noah scoured his mind for any other clues Sam could have dropped in conversation.

The day dragged on like a slug making its way through molasses. He thought about going by Maggie's Café for a takeout, or else picking up some lunch meat and bread at the grocery store and staying in the speakeasy that night. But after Sam didn't show up at the bookstore for another day, he decided to go home. Everywhere he turned, memories of her flashed through his mind. He had kept his phone ringer on loud and clipped it to his belt just in case she called, but it hadn't happened.

When he got home to the trailer, he made himself two pieces of toast and an omelet with the last three eggs left in his fridge, but he could only eat half of it and tossed the rest in the trash. He tried to think up an excuse to call Kathleen again, but not a blessed thing came to mind. If Sam needed time, then he should give it to her.

If she needs time to heal, maybe I do too, he thought as he sat beside the collection of his things Laura had left on his couch. He stared at the box for several minutes and with a long sigh began to rummage through it—hopefully to settle the past once and for all.

The toothbrush he had kept at Laura's went directly into the trash along with half a bottle of Stetson. He remembered the first morning they spent together in an expensive hotel in Dallas. She had watched him shave and then frowned when he opened that same bottle.

"You could wear something that doesn't smell like an eighty-year-old cowboy, you know."

After that he thought about buying a different kind, but he couldn't make himself do it. The scent was what his grandfather wore, and he had given him a bottle when he first taught him the proper way to shave. He could still feel his grandpa's hands guiding him that morning, and the memory put a smile on his face.

The next thing he picked up was a long, narrow velvet box with a sapphire and diamond necklace inside. He had given that to her for Christmas the first year they were together. The blue stones reminded him of her eyes. Not once had he seen her wear it or the matching ring that he had given her for Valentine's Day. She had worn the earrings only one time when they went out to dinner and a play in Dallas. Noah was a tad shocked Laura had given back all the jewelry that he had given during their relationship. He'd thought she'd keep them, maybe pawn them.

"What do I do with this stuff?" he muttered when he had lined up more velvet-covered boxes on the bed. A brooch that she had marked in one of her many magazines and a diamond tennis bracelet she wanted for the courthouse Christmas party last year, along with several thousand dollars' worth of more jewelry.

He shoved all of them into the drawer of the nightstand. "I'll have a silent auction and donate all the money to the school or sell them and send the money as a wedding gift if Surfer Man pops the question."

The rest of the stuff went right back into the box and was promptly carried out to the trash dumpster. The purging of his past made him wonder if the time would ever come when Sam would leave things at his place? Or would she too be ashamed that he lived in something so humble? Laura couldn't stand that he had moved into a trailer when he moved out of the Carter home, but would Sam mind? He might be able to ask her if Kathleen would ever let him talk to her again. Noah's brain ran a million miles a minute. When would he be able to explain everything to Sam?

Noah slept fitfully that night, tossing and turning, stuck in the loop of the same nightmare that kept recurring over and over again. In the dream, he made his way to the Rose Garden, planning to sit on the porch until Sam came out to talk to him, or else he would die of starvation waiting on her. He had armed himself with a bag of books in one hand and a sword in the other. If Jack was anywhere around, he intended to use the sword to protect Sam.

As the house came into view, he realized Jack would be the least of his problems. The rose bushes had grown thorns the size of steak knives and covered the cobblestone walkway with dense brambles, creating a wall of needle points between him and the house. The vines seemed to have minds of their own as they twisted around the front door and the windows on the lower floor. There was no way Sam could get outside and no way for him to get to her either. Tossing the bag of books to the ground, Noah pulled back his sword and began hacking away at the bushes until a noise above him caught his attention and he looked up. Sam stood unmoving in the tiny attic window of Rose Garden, tears streaming down her pained face.

Just as he had started making progress, the bushes would twist and move and quickly fill back in the wounded areas in its defense. Noah's arms got heavier and heavier, every swing of the sword now taking more from him as the blade dulled to the sharpness of a butter knife. He sucked in a breath and leaned against the hilt of the weapon as he looked up. But Sam wasn't there in the attic window anymore. Instead, there stood Jack, a creepily wide grin on his face, staring down at Noah as he panted.

"Gotcha!" Jack said with one of his leering grins.

Noah launched up in a cold sweat, ending the nightmare with a bang. His heart thumped so hard in his chest that he couldn't breathe for a moment. After inhaling several times, he slung his legs over the side of the bed, and with a mouth that felt as if it had been swabbed out with cotton balls, he made his way to the kitchen for a glass of water.

Something hung over him like an ominous omen in his nightmare. *I need to see her, just to make sure she's okay.*

Thank God the next day was when the committee planned to stuff the Easter eggs.

Noah compiled some books for all three women, taking extra care with what he picked out for Sam, and headed for the Rose

Garden—just a tad bit early. He may only get to see her through a room of other folks, but at least he could lay eyes on her. That's all he wanted at that point. Her absence was a daily ache he couldn't stomach much longer.

Noah thought it strange that there were no vehicles parked anywhere when he pulled up, but maybe he was the first one to arrive, so his plan to leave early had worked. He got out of his truck, picked up the bag, and was halfway to the porch when Kathleen opened the door and stepped out.

"Oh, I should have called you today, but we got busy. The Key Club at the school all met at the chamber of commerce office and stuffed the eggs yesterday. They needed to do something for the community, so I gave them that job."

"I always looked forward to helping with that," Noah said, not knowing what else to say.

"So did I," Kathleen said. "We had such a good time, but the kids needed something for the community outreach sector of the club, and it helps connect them with their town by acts of service. Maybe next year."

"Is Sam around?" Noah asked cautiously.

"She's still not feeling her best," Kathleen answered flatly.

"Do we need to take her to the hospital?"

"No, Noah, nothing like that."

"Well what's wrong, then, Kathleen? Why won't she see me?"

"Noah, it ain't my story to tell. Just be patient. I'll tell her that you called, and I'll bring her the books for you. But she needs to figure her own stuff out right now, just like you do."

Noah nodded stiffly and handed the bag to Kathleen. "I put in a few cowboy books, just in case she feels like reading something different. Tell her that I miss her and I've read some of the books she likes. And tell her that I get why she reads them. I see the silver lining too now that I've read a few of the ones that she brought back."

Kathleen nodded. "I'll let her know, but at my discretion. Thank you for bringing these up. Will we see you tomorrow morning at the sunrise service?"

"Of course."

"I'll see you then, thank you again." Kathleen waved and went back inside, a surge of sadness hitting Noah as the wooden door clicked shut in front of him.

Noah walked back out to the middle of the cobblestone walkway and squinted at the attic window. Sam wasn't there, but he saw a curtain flutter on the second floor. Then in his peripheral vision he caught movement coming from near his truck and swung around, expecting to see Sam, but it was Jack.

"What are you doing here, Jack?" Noah's voice was low.

"I reckon I could ask you the same, couldn't I?" Jack leaned against the metal side of Noah's Ford truck and smiled up at Noah as he picked at his dirty nails with a pocketknife.

"I was checking in on Sam. Kathleen said she's been sick."

"Sick? That's what the old coot told you?" Jack snarled and kept cleaning his nails.

Noah didn't answer but just straightened his shoulders and waited.

"While you've been getting cucked by Laura, I've been making sure Sam wasn't too lonely out here. She's a mighty good girl, Noah, and she deserves to be taken real good care of." The way Jack accentuated certain words in that last sentence made Noah want to wipe the dirty smirk off the man's face with his fist.

"What does Kara think about you going after Sam?"

"What do I care?" Jack shrugged and continued cleaning his nails while talking. "It seems your run of luck is over, buddy, and mine's just beginning. Laura finally realized how low she had fallen by dating you. Sam is giving me a chance, and now you're all alone. Poor pitiful Noah—always the victim."

"I'd rather be seen as a victim than a predator," Noah snapped back.

Jack's knife stopped moving, and he glared at Noah. "What did you call me?"

"I heard what you did to Laura, about all the bruises on her after she broke it off more than once. I ain't letting you get close to Sam."

Jack laughed at this and stood taller. "You're a little too late."

Noah's gut twisted, and he took a step closer to Jack.

Jack raised the knife, and pure evil shot from his eyes.

"Are you threatening me right now?" Noah was surprised when Jack leveled the knife at him. Sure, Jack had kicked and punched Noah when they were kids, but he'd never pulled a weapon out on the playground.

"Of course not." Jack grinned and angled the blade back and forth a bit so it glinted in the sunlight between them as he came closer and closer, right up until the tip of the knife brushed the front of Noah's shirt. "I'm just getting my point across, Carter. You're too late and a woman short. You need to keep to yourself and away from here. Sam doesn't need any of your damn books or your company, so you can scurry on to your shop and lick your wounds there."

"I'm not going to let you hurt her." Noah's face was hard steel, anger having etched his facial features into stern lines.

"Yeah? And how the hell are you gonna stop me?" Jack pushed the knife a bit closer.

Noah could feel the sharpness of the blade through the cotton of his shirt. Jack wouldn't be crazy enough to stab him, would he?

Noah didn't honestly know the answer to that question, but he couldn't back down now. Not if Jack really was getting closer to Sam and could hurt her.

Just then, a car came bustling up the drive and swung out to park in the lot at the B&B. Jack took an abrupt step back before snapping the switchblade back in and slipping it in his pocket.

The family of three parked and started unloading from their minivan.

"Kathleen told you that you weren't allowed here years ago." Noah lowered his voice so the family couldn't hear.

"Times change," Jack whispered back snidely, shrugged, and then spoke up. "Now, I'm gonna help this lovely couple in with their bags, and you should get on back to your books."

Jack waved at Noah in fake niceness and turned to the grateful family to help them walk their baggage to the door.

Noah didn't see Kathleen's response to Jack standing on the threshold with the family's luggage in tow. He didn't want to know. Maybe they *had* made nice, and Kathleen finally approved of Jack even after everything he'd done in the past, but that thought formed new knots in Noah's stomach.

Noah pulled out of the B&B's parking area and headed back into town. If he went home, he would just pace around the trailer until sunrise. He headed to the bookshop, but after a few hours, hunger gnawed at him and no work was getting done so he called Maggie's.

"Justine, are y'all busy right now?" he asked, glad that she had answered the phone. "I'm starving, but I don't want to be interrogated today."

"Howdy there, neighbor, the coast is relatively clear. There's one table of old biddies from the Presbyterian Church, but other than that, we're dead here."

Noah drove to the café and parked in the rear and kept his head down as he headed to the back booth. Justine had already set a cup of coffee out for him, and Noah was touched by the gesture. Justine was one of the most thoughtful humans Noah could remember from his childhood. He clung to her as a child in nursery on Sunday mornings when his parents were in the chapel for a sermon. She had even become a sort of surrogate mother after losing his own and especially since Laura had come into his life.

Justine appeared with a glass of water and a menu. "Do you know what you wanna eat?"

"The catfish dinner with hush puppies and collards, and if there's any pecan pie left, I'd like a slice of that too," he answered.

Justine nodded and hurried away to put the order in. Noah leaned back and closed his eyes. Folks tend to think that they are in a soundproof cage when they sit down in a booth. He supposed that Ramona Edgewood, Annie Lawrence, and Jane Weathersby hadn't seen him walk in because he found himself unable to not hear what was going on in their gossip circle two booths down. Ramona was deaf in one ear and slowly losing hearing in her other, so Annie and Jane had to practically shout to keep the vein of conversation open.

"You hear about Justine's girl?"

"Lord yes. I'd be just up in arms about it if I were Justine. She is holding it together, poor dear."

"I heard the man Laura stepped off with looks like Fabio," Annie crowed. "Some big hunk of a man. I heard he surfs."

"Could we find him on Facebook, you think?" Ramona asked.

The three women broke into a chorus of giggles at the question.

"And just about the time Laura Henton gets out of Dodge, I've got wind that Jack Reynolds has set his eye on a girl at the Rose Garden. He's after that woman Kathleen and Loretta took in," Jane added.

"I thought he liked 'em fast. I heard that girl is a bookworm. I doubt Kathleen lets him in the door anymore," Annie said.

"Maybe he's ready to settle down," Ramona answered.

"Boys like Jack don't settle down for one woman. I hope she's smart enough to . . ."

Annie's ringtone was a cat meowing, making Ramona ask, "Do you hear something?"

Annie pointed to her phone. "It's just my ringtone, one second," she yelled, followed by a softer, "Hello."

Noah heard a few uh-huhs before Annie raised her voice again to tell the women, "Loretta just rang. She confirmed it. Jack is coming round again, and Kathleen don't like it, not even a little bit. He won't seem to leave that girl be. Also, she asked if anyone had the coupon for ground chuck this week from the Sunday paper."

The conversation slingshot itself to the cost of milk and cheese before coming back to the gossip as Justine came up to ask the ladies if they would like any dessert.

"Raspberry tea and a slice of coconut pie for each of us," Annie answered. "And, Justine, we are worried sick about you. How are you holding up?"

"Let me grab a to-go order real quick, and I'll come back and tell you all about it." Justine gave them a conspiratorial wink and turned back to the kitchen. That seemed to make the women giddy.

Justine left Noah's eyesight for a moment but quickly arrived back at his booth with a to-go bag in tow and said, "The back door's unlocked if you wanna sneak out, I'm gonna try and be good press where I can."

"I haven't paid yet."

"I got it! Now, go!"

The woman was truly a saint. There was no doubting that. Noah slipped back to the speakeasy with his dinner and sat in the quiet, not tasting his food but chewing on what Kathleen had said about Sam.

CHAPTER NINE

MAMAS, DON'T LET YOUR BABIES GROW UP TO LOVE COWBOYS

Sam reckoned it was time to put her foot down with Buster to get him to focus on helping her locate a car. She had been in Homestead for over two months now, and she had scoured newsletters and scrolled online fruitlessly for a new Patsy. Those two months had been the longest she had gone without a car since she got her license at sixteen, but somehow it hadn't seemed to mess with her day-to-day very much. How long it was taking to find her a reasonably priced Mustang hadn't been too big of a deal until her mama had enforced the Mother's Day visit as imperative. The two hundred plus miles between Rosepine and Homestead loomed on the horizon of the coming weekend.

Her mother had an uncanny way of calling right when Sam felt the most dismal and would beg Sam by the end of the call to come on home. As if by fate, her cell phone rang as she reached the end of the sidewalk that evening. Sam stopped and pulled it from her back pocket with a huff. It was another night when Nibbler refused to leave the couch cushion, and Sam had left his leash hanging in the kitchen when she pulled her tennis shoes on.

She was in the middle of her run and didn't want to pause the song in her headphones or her workout, but if she didn't, then Wanette would call the Rose Garden next. She and Kathleen had become what Sam referred to as phone pen pals over the past couple months. If Kathleen didn't answer, well then, Wanette would call Everbloom next, and Sam wanted to avoid that.

She put on her best cheerful voice and answered, "Hey, Mama, how are you?"

"When you left, we expected you to be gone three months. Three months and no more, mind you. The deal was that you would be home for Mother's Day. Tomorrow's Easter, which means you'll have roughly two weeks before I expect you to be home." Wanette annunciated each syllable slowly.

"I know." Sam sighed. "Sorry, I should've visited sooner than now. But I still don't have a car, Mama. I guess I could borrow Kathleen's for a weekend, but I feel bad asking."

"Well, I suggest you either ask her or just expect your daddy up there in a dozen days to pick you up and drive you home. I can live without my children on most holidays, but all three of you girls have always been home to celebrate Mother's Day with me. This is *my* holiday. I need you home with me, and I refuse to let Chase and Liza Beth rob me of my time with you this year." Wanette's tone left no wiggle room for argument.

"Yes, ma'am. I understand," Sam said. "Why are you blaming them?"

"If it hadn't been for them, you might still be living in Rosepine. You might have come to your senses and kicked Chase out of your life soon enough, but you wouldn't have run so far away to lick your wounds and whine. You will be home for Mother's Day weekend. Do you understand me?" Wanette doubled down.

"I promise I will do my best," Sam said.

"This time your best isn't good enough. You are coming home, Samantha. I have to go now. I love you." Wanette ended the call.

The positive side of her mother being short was that Sam had no time to slip up and tell her about Jack. It's not like she had planned anything to happen, but Jack had been relentless. The morning after she puked on his boots, Sam had really thought she had run him off for good. But there he was, knocking on the back door around four in the afternoon with burgers and fries in a grease-soaked bag in one hand and a large Coke with two straws in the other. He had gotten extra onions on her burger, and she marveled at first at how sweet she thought that was. When she opened the wrapper, she gagged so badly that he had to walk a few yards away to scrape them off of her bun and onto the grass. The herbal stuff that Loretta and Kathleen had given Sam earlier had helped, but the onions that Sam had puked up had been gnarly, and she would probably never eat them again.

Since she had been wary to bring Jack inside, not quite knowing what Kathleen or Loretta would think of him showing back up after their garden talk a few hours before, they sat on the back steps together—shoulder to shoulder with their elbows on their knees, dipping fries in a communal ketchup pile on the inside of his burger wrapper while Jack told her about a car in the shop that he thought she might like.

She chewed on another fry and wondered why he had made the trek up there to see her again considering the puking situation had happened only about twelve hours ago. He talked as she ate— the greasy fries and burger tasting better than they ever had before. After they both finished their burgers, he kissed her hand and left.

Sam was totally baffled and watched as he walked back toward the auto shop. The man confused her. Sam was slowly learning that he played the role of "the gentleman" well when he wanted, and the role fit him like a good pair of Levi's.

The next day, she got a call from an unknown local number and pulled her phone to her ear. Lo and behold, when the connection went through, it was Jack's deep drawl asking her out on a date. She almost choked from surprise, first because her phone was working, second because he had gotten her number at some point from someone, and third because he was asking her out on an actual date over the phone.

She was flattered. And promptly told him no, and then he hung up. She had told Kathleen that she'd listen to her and Loretta's warnings, and Sam had no doubt that Kathleen would kill her if she went out with Jack. The two women had made her solemnly swear on a cowboy paperback in the garden that day to let cheating lying stinking dogs lie. Even Noah had warned her about Jack.

Sam knew to leave it alone, but the more she decided against it, the more Jack started showing up in her life. A visual of Loretta coming in cussing one evening when she had gotten an order to make a bouquet for Sam, per Jack and his credit card info left on the florist shop voicemail one morning.

"I ain't condoning this, Sam, and I ain't makin' an arrangement for him." Her voice was so shrill it could have cut through glass. "He's bad news, Sam."

"People can change, Loretta. I wasn't always the best person, but I grew up," Sam spoke softly, but she couldn't seem to convince Loretta to soften her heart toward Jack. And never mind Kathleen. Sam knew that was a lost cause.

"Loretta pointed at Sam as she brushed past her. "You're absolutely right. People can change. Just not Jack. You're gonna get hurt if you get too close to him. He ain't no good." The women in Sam's life were normally right when they warned her about something, and she could hear Inez's voice chime in.

Your trio of wise sages say he's no good, kid. Listen to women who know better.

Wanette had been right too. Sam was indeed hardheaded. But she swore she had good reason to be stubborn. Jack made her feel beautiful and wanted again, and she didn't think of Noah in those times. She needed a distraction, and Jack was eager to be that for her.

A day or so later, Jack called her up at the flower shop and asked her to meet him that night at Scottie's. She felt like a teenager with a dirty little secret all day because of it. She waited 'til Loretta was in bed and Kathleen was in front of her nightly Westerns, and she slipped through the kitchen and out the back door. She even made it all the way to the driveway without setting Nibbler into a barking tirade.

Jack was egotistical and wasn't the be-all and end-all in Sam's book, but he was funny. And he was hot. Any woman would agree with her there. Besides, she had never been with the bad boy before, and it was a lot of fun. She was getting quicker at running, she told herself as she ran by the moonlight-dappled path. She felt so very alive as her legs and heart pumped in double time. At the edge of town, she slowed to a walk and caught her breath before swinging open the dented metal door at Scottie's.

Her eyes lasered in on him as soon as she walked in. He leaned near the end of the bar, two shots of whiskey in his left hand, and his eyes trained on the door like he knew just when she would arrive. His face softened into a smile when their eyes met, and he held out his hand.

She felt like he had just cast a spell on her again. Between the liquor and the small talk over the next couple hours, Sam learned more about him and found him aggravatingly charming all over again. He was a good dancer, a pool shark through and through, sure, but he also was observant and didn't seem to miss a thing.

Sam felt very small and feminine next to him. He was lean but tall, and when they stood side by side and Jack flexed his arms on the rounded side of the bar, she began to see him in a whole new way. It didn't help that the night was filled with more laughter and fun than she had expected.

On the walk home, when Jack tugged her off the path, she didn't argue with his suggestion for a detour. They walked past the B&B and then on what looked like a goat's trail before a clearing opened ahead of them. Right in front of them was a small log cabin, cocooned by the cedars and pines in the middle of the meadow.

"This was my great-uncle's. We were really close, and I was his favorite when I was growing up. This was his hunting lodge back then." His voice was filled with pride.

"It's really nice back here."

He tugged on her hand. "You gotta see it up close. Come on."

When they reached the cabin, Jack pulled a key from under a red-painted rock in the mulch near the front door and waved it in front of her.

"Gotcha." He unlocked the door, flicked the lights on, and stepped back to hold the door for her.

The inside of the little cabin was wall-to-wall heart pine and stone, whitewashed mortar trimming the logs with a smattering spiderwebs in the corners. It smelled like mothballs and obviously had not been lived in for a long time. But the place felt warm and welcoming. Jack locked the door behind him and stepped up close behind her. His body felt like a stone statue. She remembered Jack saying he lived above the auto shop, so whose living room were they standing in?

"Who owns this place now? You?" Sam asked. Something in her gut told her not to turn around.

"Pretty much." Jack lowered his mouth to be level with her ear, his lips brushing against her earlobe when he spoke. "Kathleen's leaving it to me."

A bright red warning flare went off somewhere inside Sam. This must've been Thurman's. He had said it was his uncle's, *his great-uncle's*. "Does she know you come down here? Or that she's leaving it to you?"

"She doesn't have to know anything, baby." Jack nipped at her earlobe.

She tried to move away, but his arms tightened around her, wrapping her in a bear hug from behind. The realization of how vulnerable a position Sam was in hit her like a wrecking ball when his arms tightened around her like a python, and he strung kisses from her ear to her neck.

"Let me go, Jack, I don't like this."

"Aw, come on, baby, just relax." His breath was hot and heavy when he murmured against her ear, licking a trail to the outer rim of her ear and flicking his wet tongue into its hollow.

"No, Jack! Let me go." She bucked against him, but his grip tightened, and pure panic enveloped her whole body.

"Calm the hell down, just relax, you're too uptight." He was stronger than Sam could have ever imagined, and the panic turned into fight-or-flight mode. She chose the former and stomped on his steel-toed work boot, but it didn't faze him.

He growled against her neck, "Stop it, Sam."

"Let me go, and I'll stop, Jack." Her voice quavered. She really didn't want to hurt him, but if worse came to worst, she could and would.

"You're gonna do what I say, Sam. I said to be still, dammit."

"Like hell I will." She kicked back into his shin and squirmed to the right the best she could.

He let out a string of foul language and pushed her hard, sending her to the hardwood floor in front of him and knocking the breath out of her. He grinned when she gasped and tried to sit up. He made a tsking noise as he walked over to straddle her, his feet planted on either side of her thighs.

"Now that's better. You're gonna do what I say, Samantha. You might even like some of it." His words were a mixture of anger and liquor.

He dropped to his knees on either side of her hips, and Sam thrust her knee upward with as much force as she could. She hit her target, and Jack seized on the way down, a yowling high-pitched howl sending him careening, grabbing at his crotch as he folded into the fetal position. The high-pitched noise that came from him reminded her of what a wounded and dying animal might sound like. His knees locked up, leaving him moaning and curled up on his side. Sam panted as she scrambled back from him and straightened up when she realized that she was out of danger.

"You bitch," Jack groaned as he glared at her, daggers shooting from his eyes.

"Don't ever speak to me again. Don't even look at me," she spit at him, her voice cracking as she shouted the last few words over her shoulder. She unlocked the door with shaking hands and took off like a wild hare. She ran like her life depended on it. The trees were a blur as she ducked their branches, leaped over logs, and jumped over holes in the path. She was breathless and sobbing when she reached the porch and began banging on the front door with both hands. Kathleen swung the door open as Sam collapsed into her arms. Kathleen swiftly locked the door behind her and then hollered for Loretta without letting go of Sam.

"I have a gun!" Loretta squawked from the back of the house as her footsteps testified she was running toward them.

"We don't need a gun. We need tea and cake and maybe a shot of whiskey."

Kathleen led Sam to the kitchen and sat her down on a chair. Loretta grabbed a quilt from one of the settees in the living room and wrapped it around Sam's shoulders, then poured a mug half full of tea and topped it off with whiskey. She pressed it into Sam's hand. "Now talk," she said.

Kathleen's face got darker and stormier the more Sam told them what had happened. The black clouds only dissipated for a moment when Kathleen erupted into laughter at the part when Sam kneed Jack firmly in the balls.

"I knew you were tough. I didn't know you were wily too. Brava, my girl, brava."

"If there was one thing my dad taught me, it was how to fight your way out of a room. Thank God he did. I don't want to think about what Jack would've done." Sam shuddered, and her eyes began to burn again. "I really thought he had a good side after all. I was wondering if maybe the bad boy thing covered up a sweeter side. I was wrong. I was so wrong . . ." Her voice finally trailed off.

"You know what we could do, Katty," Loretta said in a low voice as she wiped her hands on a dish towel with one hip leaned against the front of the sink and her opposite leg propped up like a flamingo's.

"Hush."

"What's she talking about?" Sam asked.

Kathleen put on the kettle for more tea. "Nothing. We are not going to the woods. Sam has proven that she can take care of herself."

Loretta looked down at her thin hands and flipped them over, looking at her palms. "We could let the woods take care of him for us. Lord knows how many women we'd save the pain of knowing him, Kathleen."

"Shut it, Rett. We're doing this the right way. I'm gonna call the Lightner boy soon to tell him."

"Are you seriously telling me you'd take Jack Reynolds out in the woods and kill him for me?" Sam gasped.

Loretta's birdlike shoulders shrugged, but she didn't look up. "If he touches you, he messes with me."

Sam had known the women loved her. They had consoled her. They had guided her. They had picked at her and teased her playfully from time to time, but something about this night felt different. Like a new form of womanly protection that Sam had only felt before from her mother and sisters. A bond had been forged where you'd die for the other. Hell, you'd kill if you had to.

Kathleen's jaw was set, and her eyes flashed unspoken warnings aimed at Loretta while she dialed the phone and waited for someone to pick up on the other end until the call finally went through. "Yes, this is Kathleen Scott, I need to talk to Bobby as soon as possible."

There was a pause, and then she said, "Uh-huh, yes. It's Kathleen. We don't need fire or medical, but I need Bobby up here at Rose Garden as soon as he can get here. Jack's acting up. Okay, then. Tell him that I'll be expecting him within the hour."

Samantha was horrified to think she had to talk to a cop, but Kathleen took the lead when a big man with a badge lumbered in and sat down with the three women in the kitchen. Kathleen made a pot of midnight coffee and poured him a mug as she flawlessly relayed everything Sam had told her and occasionally looked at Sam for clarification.

"Okay, I will put all this on file. I'll also go find him and warn him that he shouldn't reach out to any of you or come out to Rose Garden again." The sheriff looked over at Sam. "Now pertaining to the physical attacks on you, would you like to press charges, ma'am?"

"No." Sam decided. "I don't want to go to court, I don't want to spend one more minute of my life thinking about the parasite. He can go to hell on his own. He don't need my help."

Sam pointed at Loretta and gave her a knowing look. Loretta zipped her lips with wide innocent eyes, and the officer smirked. "Well, if you change your mind, you can come to the station and talk to me at any point. I'll be speaking to Jack fairly soon. And I'll do my best to put the fear of the law into him for you ladies."

"Bobby, tell your family Happy Easter for us, you hear? I hate starting your Good Friday like this, but I'm grateful for good boys like you protecting us here in Homestead. Tell your mama and daddy hello for me. Who knows? I may see them at church for the sunrise service."

Kathleen pressed an Easter egg–shaped tin of cheese straws into his big hands and patted his arm as she walked him to the front door. "Oh, and if you'll let Jack know something from me, that would be grand, dear. Tell him that if he shows up near my property again, I will shoot him and drag his body over the threshold. Make that clear to him," she said in a sugary sweet voice.

Bobby's eyebrows shot all the way to the brim of his hat, but he just nodded and said, "Yes, ma'am."

When he had gone, Sam finally let out the breath she had been holding. "Sweet Jesus, Kathleen! You shouldn't joke about killing Jack to an officer. If something ever happened to him, they'd come haul you to jail first thing."

"Loretta and I changed Bobby's diapers as a baby in the First Methodist nursery. That boy was in Bubba's grade. He would sooner haul the Easter Bunny or his own granny in before he'd take me to jail. Being a withered old lady is sometimes alibi enough, Samantha." Kathleen winked to the lift.

CHAPTER TEN

BACK AGAIN

Easter came and went without an event, which was a blessing to Sam. She feared Jack would come looking for her, full of anger that they had called the cops on him. But several days went by, and Jack didn't show. Sam didn't go to church that Easter Sunday. When she asked the ladies how the service went, Kathleen remarked that Noah had walked over to their pew and asked about her after the service had ended.

But he still didn't call.

Kathleen seemed to be more militant about Sam's safety now than even her roses. She insisted that Sam take her car when she went anywhere. She had banned Sam from her nightly walks, doubling down on all measures so that Sam would never run into Jack. Sam had obeyed willingly for a few days, but there came a day that the rigid routine of only being in the florist shop or Rose Garden finally got to her.

Instead of going back to the B&B after closing the flower shop that afternoon, Sam went for a walk down the hill to the town square. She stopped at the café on the other side of the square. A pretty woman with curly blond hair led her to a booth and brought her a water with lemon.

Justice or Justine. Sam tried to remember. Her mind had stopped listening until the woman said that she was Laura's mother, then it perked right up.

"Good to meet you. I'm Sam. Uh, how is Laura doing?"

The woman's face lit up at this question. "She is doing great! They landed in Waikiki a few days ago, and they're taking the next couple weeks to explore and get a view of the land. They're actually looking at houses tomorrow." The woman beamed with the good report from her daughter, her happiness apparent.

"Well, I'm happy for her! I'm glad she got out of Homestead. Er, I mean because she didn't like it here, not like I wanted her to leave, you know what I meant." Sam hadn't meant to say it like that and blushed scarlet. She was surprised the woman shared so much, and even more surprised that Laura had just moved on from someone like Noah so quickly.

The older lady with round blue eyes folded her notepad up and stuck it back in her apron with a knowing smile. "I understood ya, honey. I'm glad for her sake that she left Homestead too."

Sam's eyes darted to her name tag again to see it said Justine. With a nicety about working on filling up her sweet tea and checking in with the kitchen on her order, Justine left Sam alone again with her thoughts.

Justine brought her more tea, slid into the booth across from her, and leaned forward as she whispered fervently, "Listen, I can't *not* tell you this and not regret it later. You need to be careful with Jack. He can be physical when he's angry. He was rough with Laura when they dated."

"Laura and Jack dated?" Sam asked, amazed that Justine was dropping whispered bombshells.

"Yes, on and off before she wised up and got with Noah. She pretends it didn't happen. She avoids him like the plague now, but he got physical with her near the end. Just please be careful."

Sam's mouth was bone dry by the time the woman finished. She reached her hand out to Justine, and said, "I know."

That was all Sam had to say for Justine's eyes to mist up. "Are you okay?"

"I'm fine. Kathleen called the cops."

Justine looked at the ceiling with her mouth set in a tight line and shook her head. "Oh thank the heavens that you are alright. I should've gone straight to Kathleen and told her what had happened back then when I heard he was after you. I just didn't want to spill Laura's secret. It should be her story to tell if she wants to."

"The sheriff has given Jack a healthy talking-to, and now his actions are on file. I appreciate you warning me though," Sam said.

Sam liked Justine from the get-go. She sent Sam on her way with a free slice of apple pie wrapped in tin foil on top of her leftovers, and Sam felt another part of Homestead instantly become homier to her.

Sam pinpointed the café as another safe space to visit with no fear of running into Jack.

Something other than Jack set Sam's mind into a whirl on the way back home. Justine had just given her a secondary confirmation that Laura had left Noah and he was officially single. A little flicker of hope came alive deep inside her, but it was probably too soon after a long-term relationship breakup to strike up their friendship again. Also, what if it wasn't Laura that made Noah change his hours? He also could have wanted the friendship to end. He had supposedly asked about Sam at church but never called. Not once.

Thinking about Noah, Sam called the bar when she realized she had left his flashlight there last week and asked Rita to drop it by Everbloom for her. And though Rita Jo seemed grouchy at this request, she begrudgingly agreed when Sam promised to have a thank-you bouquet of wildflowers and sunflowers ready for pickup tomorrow at the Rose Petal with Rita Jo's name on it.

"I noticed the sunflower tattoos down your arm and collar bone," she said sweetly.

"I'll do it," Rita Jo said, "if you will sign the card *from your secret admirer.*"

That saved Sam from a run-in with either of the men she needed to avoid for now. Two birds, one flashlight. It also saved her from going into the bar at all. She had reflected a lot about Jack since the cabin brawl. And what hindsight had made the clearest was that any time Jack Reynolds came into the picture, too much Jack Daniels followed soon after it, and the two of them had come hand in hand into her life. Aside from the physical stuff, that was reason enough to rid her life of both of them. She couldn't even think about Jack now without remembering what Justine had said about Laura. The memory of him made her sick.

Sam had reeled when the gossip about Laura cheating finally reached her at the floral shop, but she honestly didn't know if she had really believed it until now. Loretta had walked into the shop with her phone to her ear that morning. Her eyes had glittered as she listened to whatever were the newest, juiciest rumors. She came close to pacing a hole through the black-and-white tile of the shop's front display room floor and wondered what in the world had gotten her so worked up.

"Laura slept with a man at the courthouse, and they're moving to Hawaii, and now Noah is single!" she squealed so loudly that her voice could have raised the dead when she finally hung up. She had done a little dance in her pink kitten heels, tapping in a circle with her arms above her head.

"Wait . . . what?" Sam had waited for Loretta to explain before she allowed herself to feel any sense of hope. Soon after Loretta had started full tilt into the story she had heard, Jack had called the shop and distracted Sam from the Noah debacle again by inviting her to sneak out and meet him that night at Scottie's.

After that night's events and midnight dash back to Rose Garden to get away from Jack, Sam honestly hadn't thought much of the Noah situation. She was constantly looking over her shoulder and jumping at shadows in the road and was on constant high alert over the next few days. Even her sleep suffered, but the worry had so far all been for naught.

Jack did not show, and neither did Noah.

Sam's phone buzzed in her pocket as she locked up the Rose Petal Wednesday evening and slid into Kathleen's car parked behind the B&B. She bit back a moan when she realized it was her mama. There was still the better half of a week left before she had to figure out a way to get to Rosepine. Without an answer on transportation yet and the engine light flashing in the dash of Kathleen's Cadillac, she ignored the call and pushed down the guilt by promising the angel on her shoulder she would call Wanette back when she got to the Rose Garden. When her mama's picture flashed on the screen again, Samantha knew she had to answer or she'd be in big trouble.

"Is something wrong? Are you and Daddy okay?" she blurted out. Their family had an understood rule. If you call once, they can call you back. If you call twice, it's something serious. And by the tone of her mama's voice, this was indeed serious.

"I don't know how else to say this, but I had to tell you before you came home. Chase proposed. He and Liza Beth are getting married."

The world stopped.

The sun stood still.

Not even a bird sang in the tall pine trees.

"Are you still there?" Wanetta asked.

"I'm here," Sam whispered.

"Do you want details? Or do you want to just sit with this? I'm sorry, honey. I wish I didn't have to tell you, but you needed some forewarning if you're still coming into town. I hope this doesn't run you off even longer." Sam could tell from her mother's tone that she couldn't skip out on Mother's Day in Rosepine, even though now she would rather visit hell than her and Liza Beth's hometown for the weekend.

"When are they getting married?"

"An August wedding is what folks are saying. The rumor is she's knocked up, that's why all the rush."

Sam felt herself want to double over in her seat. "And you're sure of this, Mama?" Her voice was shrill, and tears dammed up in her eyes.

"It's on Facebook."

Those three words came as the last ceremonial nail in her coffin.

Wanette went on, "You're going to be just fine, Samantha. Those two deserve each other after how they did you. They'll drive each other crazy sooner or later. You keep your head on straight and don't let this get you down. He can't be trusted, and besides he'll go bald like his daddy one day anyhow, and she'll gain fifty pounds."

Sam choked on a laugh that was stuck in her throat while tears rolled down her cheeks. "I'm fine, it's fine. I gotta go though, Mama. I got another call coming in."

"Okay, well I love you, and I'm praying for you. They'll have hideous babies. You just dodged an ugly, white-trash bullet. We love you. Finish your call and go take a bath and have a good cry if you need to, but remember that everything happens for a reason. It's going to be alright. Bye, now."

Sam stared at the phone and wondered how time had moved so slowly for her here in Homestead yet so quickly back in Rosepine. She raced back to Rose Garden to seek out Loretta and Kathleen but found an empty house with a note on the kitchen counter instead of their lively chatter.

Taking a wedding delivery north of Jefferson. Won't be back till later in the evening.

She hadn't felt this alone since she had found Liza Beth and Chase in their bed and sat out in Patsy and cried until her eyes were almost swollen shut. This was the same kind of lonesome flooding in. She felt her legs finally give, and she melted onto the kitchen floor, her face in her hands as she sobbed.

She had hit a wall where she couldn't move on if she didn't cry it out and bow under the culmination of weight she had carried for half a year now. All the pain and the insecurities Chase and Liza Beth's actions had caused her to experience, the recent fear of Jack lingering around, the confusion with Noah—it was all too much.

She really lost it. At some point, maybe minutes or even hours since Sam had started crying, the phone on the wall above her rang. Sam wanted to ignore it, but considering it could be Kathleen or a customer, she wiped her face and reached for the receiver.

"Rose Garden," she said in a nasally voice, her nose stuffy from weeping.

"Sam, thank God," Noah said. "Bobby Lightner just came in to grab something for his kids and told me what happened with Jack. Are you okay? Did he hurt you?"

"Chase and Liza Beth are getting married," she wailed.

"What? Just hold on. I'm headed to the Rose Garden now. I'll be there soon." He hung up, and Sam broke into a fresh set of sobs.

In what seemed like seconds, she heard a truck slinging gravel as it braked outside and the bounding footsteps of Noah running onto the front porch. He flung the front door against the hallway wall and ran into the room, catching himself on the doorway and searching the room frantically until he saw her.

She knew she looked pathetic, but he didn't say anything. He just plopped down beside her and pulled her into his arms, rocking her a bit as she continued to let out even more racking sobs as she held on to the front of his shirt tightly and pushed her face into his chest. Memories of the time when she and Liza Beth tried on diamond rings together kept replaying.

Noah asked questions in a soft voice, but Sam could hardly answer. Even her breaths came out as gasps, and her chest tightened when she tried to breathe deeply. She didn't know how long they sat there on the kitchen floor with their arms wrapped around each other. But soon her breathing slowed, the tears ebbed, and she pulled her sticky face away from his damp shirt. He tucked a stray tendril of hair behind her ear.

She sniffed loudly and felt sheepish. "I'm sorry."

"There's nothing to be sorry for," he said. "Just breathe. You're safe."

"Thank you." She laid her head back on his chest and took a deep breath and felt her body slowly relax a bit. "Chase and Liza Beth are engaged. They're getting married by the end of summer."

"Oh?" Noah said.

"Yeah, oh." Sam sniffed again and wiped her wet face with her sleeve.

His left arm curved around her back so she could lean against him in a more comfortable way. "Talk to me and tell me all about it."

"I always thought we'd be each other's maids of honor. That was our plan." She forced her bottom lip to stop quivering. "I guess now she'll have to play nice with the other women in town who she used to call brats. I bet Chloe Harper would be thrilled to be her maid of honor after all the crap she spread about her in school, I mean, get real." She rolled her eyes. "Thank you for holding me. Sorry . . . I just felt like I couldn't breathe when I got home, and Kathleen and Loretta were gone, and it finally hit me."

"I think you were having a panic attack, and I'm speaking as someone who has had his share of them." His eyes held a forlorn expression. "I hate this is happening to you, Sam, but I am happy this isn't about Jack. I thought he had come back up here when you answered the phone and were crying." Noah's voice was soft and soothing.

"I'm sorry. I didn't mean to scare you." She reached up and cupped his cheek with her hand for just a moment and curled back into his chest.

His arms tensed around her for a beat, and his mouth turned up in a sweet smile. "Stop apologizing, Sam, I'm just happy you're okay."

It was the right time to leave his impromptu embrace, but nothing in her body would allow her to move. Noah seemed fine to stay where he was, so she rested in the curve of his arms and told him about Jack. Her story started on the fateful night she saw the light on in Everbloom, but she skipped that section, starting with the first time she went inside the bar. She would save the part about seeing him dancing with Laura for another day.

She told him of Jack's courtship, how he kept showing up, kept buying drinks, kept pressuring her even when she said no. His expressions were the same as Kathleen's as he listened. His eyebrows inched lower and closer together until she told him about knocking Jack in the privates.

That's when he tossed his head back and howled with laughter. "Where'd you learn to do that?"

"My daddy taught me lots of self-defense stuff. He was military and taught all his girls how to defend themselves."

The darkness from Noah's eyes returned. "So, he didn't hurt you? I mean, other than shoving you on the ground and trying to . . ."

"No, I got out of Dodge, or the cabin as it were, and Kathleen called the cops when I got home."

He looked up at the tin ceiling of the Rose Garden's kitchen. "Thank you, Lord."

Sam shook her head sadly and gazed up into Noah's eyes with a haunted look. "You were right, Noah. Jack isn't a good person, and I didn't listen."

"I wish I could have protected you from this. You did nothing wrong, Sam."

He looked at her with such intensity, his eyes saying something she couldn't understand.

Noah ran his thumb over her cheek and then slipped a finger under her chin. "I should've come up here sooner. I just wanted to give you time. I have missed you so much, and I have been trying my best to not think about—"

The door opened with a bang.

Sam scrambled away from Noah like they were teenagers caught in the act.

Kathleen walked in, swinging two arms full of groceries, her face cracking into a wide smile as she looked from Sam's red face to Noah sprawled on the floor beside her.

"Well, I'm glad you're here, Noah! We just grabbed fried chicken on the way home, and we got too much! Come on, and y'all help me unload the van. I got enough for an army, and I want to talk to you about something anyway, Noah, my boy. Do you have any plans this weekend?"

CHAPTER ELEVEN

WHAT MY ANGELS
THINK OF ME

Nibbler will be fine. He loves Kathleen about as much as he loves you," Loretta fussed as Sam teared up again. The dog had been with Sam every day since the day he was born. When she moved out of her parents' house, she had rented a small garage apartment in Rosepine because it was the one available place that allowed pets.

Nibbler knew her every mood, he was practically a living, breathing furry security blanket. But her sister was bringing her two shih tzus to their parents' house, and it'd be better to leave him with Kathleen and Loretta than incite a pissing competition with PomPom and Bella over Mother's Day weekend. Her mother's Persian rug would thank her after Wanette got over the disappointment of not getting to see her furry grandson.

She sat down beside him on the bedside rug that morning and scratched his ears. "I'm going to miss you, my sweet boy, but it's only for two nights. I'll be back on Monday, and I'll tell you all about the weekend. Keep Kathleen and Loretta safe until I'm back, okay?"

"Noah is parking the car," Kathleen yelled from the bottom of the staircase.

"I'll go get your thermos ready for you. I made some more coffee." Loretta scurried down the hallway in her little fluffy house slippers that Kathleen had bought her at Easter. They didn't quite match the seafoam green velvet tracksuit she wore, but that didn't seem to bother the sentimental fashionista.

Sam slipped the straps of her Vera Bradley bag over the handle of one suitcase, gave herself one last look in the mirror, and rolled her bags out into the hallway. Nibbler ran for the stairs, but she opted for the lift. When the creaking stopped, she stepped out into the kitchen and was halfway across the living room when she caught sight of Noah on his knees in front of the dog.

"I've missed you, Nibbler," he said as he scratched around the dog's ears. "No one has brought another pup in to see me since the last time you were at the shop."

The wheels of her hefty suitcase hung on the corner of a rug, reminding her of the time that it had hit the crack in the sidewalk on the first night she was in town. So much had happened since that evening. She gave it a tug, but it didn't budge. Noah popped up on his feet and lifted the whole thing up, then carried it to the foyer.

"Good morning." His eyes were warm and twinkling when they rested on her face. "How did you sleep?"

"Wonderful, you?" Sam felt like a filthy liar. She had tossed and turned all night.

"Pretty good, actually. You ready to hit the road?"

"Just about, I'm sorry you got pressured into doing this. I told Kathleen this was too much to ask."

"Hey, Kathleen brought it up," he said. "I agreed to do it, and no one twisted my arm. Besides, I had no plans. In return for my kindness, you can help me pick up some books from a vendor on the way back. I'd have to drive down to Center sometime next week anyway."

"I feel like you'd say that even if it isn't true just to make me feel better," Sam challenged.

Noah cocked one of his eyebrows up. "I would've just let you borrow one of my cars if I didn't want to be here. Maybe I want to be your chauffeur."

Sam gaped at him and snapped her mouth shut with a giggle. *One of his cars?* She wondered how many cars Noah had. She had suspected he was a truck guy, since that's all she had seen him drive before. He smiled at her and turned to face Kathleen when she walked into the house. She slapped her knees to get dirt from her hands.

"You got a pretty one out there, Noah."

"Thanks. Glad I can take her for a proper spin."

"Me too," Loretta piped in and handed Sam and Noah each a full thermos of fresh coffee. "For the ride," she said with a smile.

"You got your passport?" Kathleen asked.

"Why would I need a passport?"

"Don't pay her any mind," Loretta said. "She thinks that Texas is a country, not a state. If you leave Texas, she thinks you'll need documents to return. She's making a joke because she's afraid you won't come back."

Sam gave each of the ladies a hug. "I have to come home. You're holding Nibbler hostage."

"You better remember that if you get to wanting to stay," Kathleen said and picked up her furry prisoner. "Now get out of here so you can get on back."

Noah motioned to Sam's bag and suitcase and headed for the door with them in tow. "I'm going to put these in the car."

"I'm right behind you," Sam told him before turning back to wrap Kathleen, Nibbler, and Loretta into a big bear hug one more time. "I hate goodbyes even if they are only for a couple of days. So, I'm going to say that I'll see y'all soon enough and go on out to the truck."

Kathleen's mouth twitched like she was about to smile.

"What's so funny?" Sam asked.

Loretta chuckled and gave her a gentle shove toward the open door. "Get out of here and enjoy the weekend."

Even after all the tossing and turning last night, and all the hours she spent playing out scenarios from the night before, she felt ill-prepared for the adventure ahead of her. She had worried about what they would talk about the whole drive, but it was all for nothing.

They were as comfortable with each other as they had been that first night when she went into the bookstore to ask for directions. *Noah is like sunshine in a human*, she thought as she walked down the front steps of the Rose Garden and thought about the plan for the weekend. She reached the small side gate and pushed it open before she finally looked up to see Noah holding the passenger door of a vintage convertible open.

"Your stuff is all loaded, and the gas tank is full." He held up a worn blue baseball cap. "I brought this so your hair isn't one big knot when we get there."

Sam's feet were frozen to the ground. She had an appreciation for antique cars of any kind. Her father had planted that seed in her heart when he'd take her to car shows as a little girl. She always suspected that he had wished his third child would be a little boy. Maybe that's why he nicknamed her Sambo before she could talk.

She was grateful for whatever reasons that her father had instilled the love for vintage cars and self-defense in her at an early age. One skill had recently protected her, the other gave her the ability to love a fifties model Chrysler New Yorker when she saw one. Her dad had a poster of one in Pepto pink on his garage wall, but the one in front of Sam was a showstopper. Painted a classic pearl-snap white with a red pinstripe streak along the sides, the red leather interior glowed like it was molten in the sunlight.

"Where did you get this?" she whispered.

"It's a long story, but one worth telling," Noah answered with a grin. "Hop on in, and I'll tell you on the drive."

She took a hair tie from her pocket, whipped her red hair into a ponytail, and took the cap from Noah. She settled it on her head and pulled her hair through the hole in the back. "I cannot believe that you have one of these. Do you have any idea how much my dad is going to flip over this car? This is insane. What year is it?" Sam rambled on and on.

When she was inside, he closed the door, rounded the back of the vehicle, and slid into the driver's seat with a laugh. "Lucky guess. I only picked it for our adventure because this car reminded me of your hair. I'm glad she got up and ran first try this morning. It was meant to be."

"You picked out your car this morning to go with my hair?" she asked.

He made a U-turn and turned right at the end of the lane. "That sounded weird, huh. When my Grandpa passed, he left his estate to me, which included twelve vintage cars he had collected over the years. He said he had one for each month of the year. This is the only one that was brand-new when it came to Carter Manor. The rest are restored, but there's a story behind each one. This is May, and she was Granny's Mother's Day present in 1957. So, from the red leather to the Mother's Day memory Granny would always tell about getting the car, it felt right for our journey today."

His face held this certain achingly beautiful look when he talked about someone he loved. A lump formed in Sam's throat as she watched his expression. She swallowed a couple times and then awkwardly cleared her throat.

"What do the rest of the months look like?" she asked.

"I'll take you out to the manor and let you see for yourself sometime. Grandpa had a special climate-controlled warehouse built for his collection on the back side of the grounds."

"That's a lot of words you're spitting out here. The manor? Climate-controlled warehouse? The grounds? Did your grandpa have more money than God, or something?" Sam asked.

She tried to remember what all Noah had shared over time about his childhood but couldn't recall much. She knew the Carter name was synonymous with affluence in the little town of Homestead, and that they always had been a well-to-do family, but Noah also lived in the same trailer park Laura despised, so she was lost. Where did a climate-controlled warehouse fit between the bookshop and the trailer park?

"Carter Manor is the family home. It's a little farther down this road. I'll point it out when we go past. My mama had wanted to make it a school when I was little, so that's what I did when Grandfather passed and I had been living there all by myself. It got pretty lonely with no one else around, and I hated being alone back then. So, I moved into Pinecrest and started working on Mama's dream. It's been running as one of the top magnet schools in Texas for four years this coming fall," Noah said proudly.

At the words *this coming fall*, a mental vision of Liza Beth in white popped into Sam's head. She swallowed hard again and had almost got control when she looked up and saw Jack walking out of his auto shop and looking down at his phone. His usual strut didn't have the same swagger. Sam hoped that she had hurt him enough that he would never try to hurt her again. But she still felt a flutter of fear travel up her throat as they neared the corner where he was standing.

As if he understood, Noah turned the car to the left and cut down a side road on the way to the highway, avoiding the auto shop altogether. He gave her a knowing look and put the car into a lower gear as they cruised on the smoother section of road.

"I saw you and Laura that night. That's why I went to the bar and met up with Jack," she blurted out.

"In the bookshop?"

Sam nodded and parroted back, "In the bookshop."

He was silent for a moment, then said, "I thought I saw you, but I told myself I was imagining it."

"Well, I scrambled because I felt like a Peeping Tom. I was just walking past, and I wasn't trying to step in on a romantic moment."

"It wasn't a romantic moment," Noah assured. "But I understand that it may have looked like it. I hate that you saw that and I couldn't explain it to you."

"You could've called me and explained it."

Noah looked over at her and seemed confused. "I did, well I tried."

Sam crossed her arms and stared straight ahead out the windshield. "No, you didn't."

"Yes so I did. I told Kathleen to give you my number, and she said she would."

"You're saying Kathleen lied to me?"

Noah sighed in exasperation. "No, Sam, I'm not saying that at all. Kathleen always has her hands full up there, and she could've forgotten to tell you, but what I am saying is that I know I called you. I also know you didn't call me because I've been keeping my phone on me nonstop, hoping that I'd hear from you."

"Well, why didn't you visit then when you didn't hear from me?"

"I did!" Noah seemed equal parts baffled and frustrated at this point. "Is Kathleen against me? Why the hell didn't she tell you I called? Or that I came over and she turned me away?"

"I don't know! I've had a lot on my mind!" She threw her hands up and slapped them back down before taking a slow breath. "Deep down, I wanted to talk to you, Noah. I kept waiting to see if *you'd* show up."

Noah reached his right hand over and laid it on top of hers, squeezing her hand softly. He slowed to a stop at the next red light and looked over intently at her. "If I had known, I would have waited on the porch until you wanted to see me."

Well, well, well! the devil and the angel on her shoulders whispered at the same time and seemed pleasantly miffed by his answer. Other than that, they both were as much at a loss for words as Sam, and she was relieved when Noah butted in and pointed at her side window.

"That is Carter Manor up there," he said.

Sam followed his finger and spotted a house that would make Rose Garden look like a child's playhouse by comparison. The looming home had a wide expanse of grounds around it, bounding green lawns and manicured hedges with clusters of magnolia trees as old as the house nestled in pockets along the property.

"You grew up there?" Sam wondered what living in something as magnificent as that would have been like.

"Yep, I moved out once my grandpa passed and I finished going through his stuff. It stopped feeling like home when he was gone. So, I had it renovated into classrooms with a cafeteria on the main floor like my mom had imagined it. I kept the bedrooms on the top floors and redid the ballroom to use as an activity room or study hall, depending on the day."

"Were you an only kid when you grew up there?"

"Yes. It's nice to go back now and hear the halls filled with voices. It's how a house like that should stay—full of life." His sad expression changed when he smiled. "The warehouse where the cars are kept is on the back fifty acres. I can show it to you another time, and we can spend a whole day joyriding if you want."

Sam had a one-track mind, and cars weren't on it right then. Like a bloodhound on a scent, she asked, "What were y'all celebrating by dancing that night?"

"I wanted us to dance to the little radio I have in there. We did that the first time I took her to the bookstore, right at the beginning of our relationship. It seemed fitting to dance."

"If I had just found out my partner had cheated on me, which I have experienced before and am still reeling from, I wouldn't be too willing to slow dance with him or her."

"Maybe it was an odd request, but it fit the end of our relationship. I wish she had told me sooner, of course, but I don't hold any ill will toward her. I'm glad she found her happiness." He looked down, flexed his hands on the wheel, and then concentrated back at the road. "I've learned over the past few years that you can love someone and not be truly in love with them. And Laura and I had been that way for a long time at that point. So, I'm grateful she set me free, so that now I can be with my person."

Sam kept her eyes straight ahead though she could feel Noah's eyes on her. She was thrilled at that last sentence, but much too terrified to meet his gaze. Noah must have sensed her discomfort and quickly put his fingers on the dial. "So, there's three stations to pick from if you want music. I hope you either like old country or nineties alternative, because it's either that or the Pentecostal channel."

She giggled and finally turned to meet his eyes.

"I'm glad Kathleen pressured you into driving me to Rosepine," Sam said.

"Me too, Sam." He flashed a brilliant grin.

On the drive back to Rosepine, their conversation touched on all the subjects under the sun except what exactly Noah had been about to tell her on the kitchen floor last night before Kathleen bustled in. Sam still hadn't gotten an answer there, and she really wanted to know. But talking about the past, life in general, music, and even random road signs never seemed to lull as the miles passed.

Sam started getting antsy when they passed the sign announcing that Rosepine was five miles farther. She held her hands in her lap to keep from fidgeting. The drive had gone by quicker than she had realized, but just the idea of being home dragged Liza Beth and Chase to the front of her thoughts. Her mother had planned the whole weekend so she wouldn't even see Chase and Liza Beth until tomorrow. Still, she wasn't sure that she wouldn't bail on the Sunday service to get out of seeing the "happy couple."

"Okay, give me directions to your house," Noah said.

"Just keep going straight through town, stay left at the fork. It's not far. Daddy has a hobby farm with a few chickens and a garden out front too now that he is retired," she told him.

"Retired? My dad would only be fifty-seven if he was living," Noah said more to himself than Sam. "How old are your parents?"

"Make the next left into that lane lined with pecan trees," she said. "I'm one of those oops babies who came along later in life. I have two older sisters. One is forty and one is forty-five. My mama is a retired nurse and almost seventy, but don't you dare tell her that I told her age. Daddy's retired military and turned seventy-two at the top of this year."

"I promise not to let it slip when I drop you off that I know your mother's age, I would like for her to like me."

"She'll love you," Sam assured him without blinking. "I hope you hadn't planned on dropping me and rushing on to your hotel room. When Daddy sees this car, he's going to want to talk all about it and look over every inch of her. He's where I get my love for older models, and he is going to be giddy to see this beauty. Then he'll want to show us both what he's growing in his garden this season, and by then, Mama will insist you stay for lunch since it'll be noon."

Noah shot a mischievous grin over toward her. "I would have dressed up if I'd known I was meeting the parents."

"You look just fine to me," she told him with an impish grin. "May I ask what happened to your parents? You said you were raised by your grandfather mostly."

"I was. My parents had a place in the Rockies that they liked to fly to for the occasional weekend. My dad was a good pilot and had owned the plane for years. But a storm hit, and their plane went down on one of their flights up to the cabin. I was with my grandfather when it happened, and he kept me from that day on at Carter Manor."

"How old were you when this happened?" Sam's voice almost broke.

"I was eight."

A wave of sadness washed through her for the little boy that Noah once was. No wonder his grandfather's death affected him so deeply. When Noah had lost him, he also lost the last connection he had to his parents.

"I'm so sorry, Noah, I can't imagine."

"It's okay now. I didn't really process the grief of losing them till Grandpa was gone too. He kept them alive by telling stories nonstop, which was a huge blessing during my growing-up years. He had a story about them for every momentous occasion, and for his cars too. He told incredible stories."

"I would really love to hear some of those stories sometime," Sam said softly.

"I appreciate that. You would've liked my parents if you had met them, and they would have loved you."

"If they were anything like you, I'm sure I would have."

He parked in a circle drive in front of a two-story white house with black shutters and a barn red door. Before he could get out of the vehicle, a woman ran down the porch steps and grabbed Sam in a hug before she was even out of the car.

"I'm so glad you are home," she said. "I needed all my girls this weekend. You kids come on inside. Dinner is ready to be put on the table. We'll have some time with just the four of us. The rest of the family that can make it are coming for supper tonight or coming over right after church tomorrow. Paul is going to grill for that. Well, don't just sit there, Samantha. Get out. Your dad was putting on his shoes, and he will be here in a minute."

Sam swung the car door open seconds before her father barreled off the porch, grabbed her in a fierce hug, and twirled her around. "This is a good day. My Sambo is home."

She was dizzy when he set her feet on the ground. "Mama and Daddy, I want y'all to meet Noah Carter. Noah, this is my father, Paul, and my mama, Wanette."

"Very high praise precedes you, Mr. Carter." Paul stuck out his hand, and Noah took it in his in a firm shake. "Kathleen already told us lots of good things about you, but she completely left out any mention of you driving this beauty. Let's get your things in the house so that my bride's happy, and then I want to hear all about this vehicle. I haven't seen one in this condition in years, not even at a car show."

"I'm just Noah, not Mr. Carter. The blue suitcase is hers, and the duffel bag." Noah came around to help Wanette as she pulled all the bags from the trunk. "I'll keep mine in here. I found a hotel room about five miles up the road. I plan to get out of y'all's hair so you can spend some good quality time with your girl."

"Well, you *had* reservations, Noah." Paul chuckled. "But unless you want to bring a bedbug infestation back to all of Homestead, you'll let me call Joann and get her to cancel and refund it for you. The local news just wrote up a front-page article on the bedbug problem they're having here in Rosepine at the motels around. There's five bedrooms upstairs, and there's no kids in this house to use them. Please, let us keep you bug-free while you're here."

"I've already got a room ready," Wanette said.

"I truly can't impose. I can find another hotel and give y'all some privacy . . ." Noah started.

Sam's father cut him off, pulling the handle of Sam's suitcase up a step and rolling it toward the house. "Son, it ain't worth arguing with my bride. She never loses, and I have nearly fifty years of marriage to prove it. Besides, the whole town of Homestead will thank you for not bringing that super bug back home. Is this all you brought, Sambo? You left with a helluva lot more."

"I did, Daddy, but I'm going home on Sunday," she reminded her father.

"Well, we can ship it all in if you change your mind," Paul grumbled. "I thought for sure we could talk you into coming back to Rosepine, and what's this about calling somewhere else home?"

"They're holding Nibbler hostage so that I'll come back, so I gotta go back at some point." Sam chuckled.

"Are you sure about me staying here?" Noah whispered to Sam. "I would never want you to feel awkward or uncomfortable."

"I'm fine with it," she said out the corner of her mouth, "but you will sure enough be ready for peace and quiet by the time we go back home. As an only child, this shall be an experience you will never forget."

Noah smiled down at her. "I like that you are calling Homestead your home."

"Me too," she said with a responding smile.

Paul parked Sam's suitcase at the base of the staircase. "Let's go have some lunch or dinner, or whatever you kids call it these days. Then I want to go outside and talk about that Chrysler. Be sure to eat real good Noah, or else Wanetta will think you don't like her cooking."

Sam led him into the dining room and felt a twinge of girlish giddiness zing through her when she saw that her mother had set the table so that she and Noah were sitting right next to each other. "You need any help, Mama?"

"I never turn down help. You guys go ahead and sit down. We'll bring in the soup and sandwiches," Wanette answered.

The moment both women were in the kitchen, Wanette smiled breathlessly. "Well, he's a looker. Kathleen told us all about his upbringing and his bookshop. A family with no money is hard, but money with no family is downright sad. She says that he's the nicest guy. Y'all complement each other well and match when you are standing side by side. I see why you fell for him."

"Mama, we aren't like that," Sam whispered feverishly and pulled her mother to the far side of the kitchen. "Not yet. He just got out of something, I just got out of something. I think he likes me, but I don't know just yet. Please, please, please." Her eyes misted as she grabbed her mother's hands. "Don't say anything about us dating around him. Kathleen is putting the cart before the horse. I don't even know if he really likes me."

"Oh, really?" Wanette smiled. "Well, I suppose we should finish getting lunch ready and head back in there. I have got questions I need to ask. Grab the sandwiches from the fridge. I got the soup."

Sam tried to hold back a moan as her mother beamed at her from the other side of the counter and carried a slow cooker into the dining room.

"I'm really glad you're surviving." Sam glanced over at Noah on the way to church on Sunday morning. "It's probably been a very crazy weekend so far."

"This has been the most wonderful weekend I've had in years," Noah admitted. "I really like your family. I can feel the love that y'all have for each other."

"My brothers-in-law and nephews didn't bore you to death with all that car talk last night, did they?" she asked.

"No, we talked about other things too—barbecuing, books, braces," he answered with a genuine grin. "I feel like I fell into a gold mine with so many folks around me that are well read. That alone made last night's festivities easy-peasy to navigate, but you seem a bit nervous this morning."

Noah's eyes flickered across her form and the green satin dress that covered it. His voice sounded a little hoarse when he said, "That color looks really nice on you. Green suits you."

"Thank you." A blush climbed from her neck to her cheek. "I appreciate that, Noah. I'm fine. I'll be fine, it's just that . . . we're pulling into the parking lot now, and I feel jumpy thinking about Chase and Liza Beth being at church."

"They may be. But you're not alone in this. I'm here. Your family is here. You have a lot of support." Noah's tone seemed to be a resounding promise. "No one from your past has any hold on you now, Sam. No one gets to upset the present. We live and we love, and we let go of what isn't ours."

She scooted over closer to him on the bench seat and laid her head on his shoulder. He used his left hand to spin the car into a parking spot near the back entrance of the church and close to Wanette's Tahoe.

"You know, you could be a motivational speaker. I would pay to hear you speak at lecture halls," she whispered.

"Or I could be your boyfriend and just talk to you for free?"

The women in Sam's family may all have enhanced Spidey senses about men, but they also all had the absolute worst timing. Sam was about to answer when Wanette knocked on the window. Before Sam rolled it down, she caught Noah's face in her hands, squishing his cheeks together and holding him face-to-face.

"We're gonna need to get to the bottom of this and talk this out later, okay?" She was as breathless as if she had just run a marathon.

"Yes," was all he replied before Wanette's voice sounded again and the two lovebirds exited the car per her request. Sam thought she saw the back of Liza Beth's head in the procession of people walking into the chapel, but she didn't know for sure. Her hair looked shorter than it had been in February if that was her, maybe even a shade lighter. Noah slipped his hand into hers and supplied a steady, solid source of warmth to her jitters until they found their family's regular pew. They visited with the surrounding congregation until the music started and they were asked to stand to sing.

The sermon Reverend Jimmy Stubbs had prepared was about forgiveness. It centered on the art of letting oneself forgive and thus be forgiven in the process. And it felt like no coincidence that the sun outside the stained-glass windows sent a shining red beacon of light onto Liza Beth and Chase in the middle pew of the third row as the message of forgiveness rang through the room.

Sam was tired of carrying the burden of hatred and anger. Right there with her family and a wonderful man beside her, all who had encouraged her to not let her past define her any longer, seemed like a good time to forgive Liza Beth Mason and Chase Warner.

And that's what she did. She said her own little prayer the next time the congregation bowed their heads. She started by asking the Lord to help her forgive them both. She prayed for the Lord to bless them and to also pour his love on her and Noah as well.

Surround me with good godly people as I wait for my perfect person to come along. Give me signs that I find him, and if it's Noah, that will be awesome.

It couldn't have been a coincidence when Noah squeezed her hand. When the prayer ended, Sam blinked back tears and felt at least a hundred pounds lighter. The sun seemed to readjust itself, and a ray of purple watercolor light flowed down upon her and Noah right there in the pew beside her parents.

You're closer than you think to your happily ever after, child. Her old friend's voice sounded like it came from her former pew across the aisle.

Sam wished Inez would be sitting there, a smile on her face, watching her with small blinking eyes as she shared with Sam some wise ad lib that solved half of the world's problems. But Inez had been an old woman when Sam was a child, and time didn't slow down for anyone. Inez hadn't sat in what Sam thought of as *her pew* in almost a decade. But her voice lingered in Sam's head long after the notes of butterscotch and warm wool from her coat pockets had faded.

I'm moving on, Inez, I wish you could see it, she murmured silently to her elderly friend's soul. *And please don't ever stop guiding me. I need all the angels I can get.*

The church sang a few songs together, and they had a baby dedication before the service concluded and Sam left Noah with her family and rushed downstairs to the ladies' room located directly under the chapel. She was finished and washing her hands when Liza Beth walked in and gasped so audibly it made Sam jump.

"Oh my God, Sam."

Sam stopped washing her hands for a moment, then thought again and lathered more soap into her hands and kept scrubbing. She kept her tone light and happy. "Hey, Liza Beth. I hear congrats are in order."

"I-I'm so sorry, Sam, I never got to tell you how bad I felt. It tore me up for months after, and I just wanted to tell you that I would never have done . . ."

"I forgive you." The single sentence rang out over the running water and cut Liza Beth off.

"What?"

"I forgive you. I have finally seen how love can make someone act. It can drive you truly crazy. I get it. And I want you to know that I forgive you, Liza Beth. Tell Chase I forgive him too, and I wish you both many years of happiness." Sam shut off the water and patted her now steadier hands down with a paper towel and tossed it in the trash can beside Liza Beth.

Liza Beth just whimpered and stared at Sam as she walked out of the bathroom. Seconds later, Sam could hear wailing in the women's restroom—barely audible through the thick wooden floors of the First Baptist Church on such a busy Sunday morning.

She went back upstairs, scanned the room, and saw an absent-minded Chase, looking around and holding Liza Beth's hot pink purse for her. Sam's stomach didn't drop. Her heart didn't stop, but instead, she looked at the man she had told herself for years she would marry one day, and she felt absolutely nothing.

The discovery felt like a rush of caffeine, and she kept her eyes moving around the room until she found Noah, standing with her parents, shaking the preacher's hand near the door as the line of churchgoers slowly disappeared out onto the street.

Noah spotted her after she had him and cut a line toward her through the crowd. "Hey, from the look on your face, it looks like you have a juicy story that I reckon I'll need to wait to get updated on. Are you ready for lunch?"

"I do have a story for you. I'll tell you all about it on the way home, and yes, I'm starving. I have finally forgiven, and now it's time to forget."

CHAPTER TWELVE

BREAKING DISHES

Loretta fanned at her face and sank down into a kitchen chair. "Lord, it's hotter than a barbed wire fence in hell out there. I vote that we watch the fireworks in air-conditioned comfort from my bedroom window and take our usual bottle of champagne up there to celebrate, Katty."

Sam brought three tall glasses of sweet tea to the table and took a sip from one before setting it at her regular place. "Enjoy the AC for me. Noah is picking me up after we're done snacking, and he's taking me to the football stands to watch the show."

Kathleen set a charcuterie tray in the middle of the table. "I hope you kids have fun. There's been a new light about you recently, Samantha. I'm glad to see that trip to Louisiana for Mother's Day did your heart so much good."

"Okay, spill it. What really happened on that trip? Did y'all screw?" Loretta layered tiny cold cuts, cheese, and crackers on her saucer with gusto.

Sam giggled at the old woman's frankness. "No, Loretta! I told you everything already. He soared through the weekend with flying colors. My family fell in love with him. My sisters and my niece could eat him with a spoon, and they have already reminded me dozens of times how wonderful he is. Anna's and Kate's husbands and Daddy also thought he had just hung the moon between his car collection and obsessive amount of random World War II knowledge." She stopped and took a sip of tea.

"I'm jealous that he got to meet them all before me and Retta did," Kathleen said, "but go on and tell us again."

"And even better, I think Noah enjoyed it as much as they did. Daddy kept on saying that Pawpaw would have loved him, and I agreed. He just meshed, like he had been part of our family all along. It was a happy, perfect, but slightly angsty weekend because he hinted at wanting to be my boyfriend, but every time he got close to spilling, someone interrupted us."

"And he didn't kiss you?" Kathleen asked.

Good Lord! At my age, I shouldn't blush at the mention of that kiss.

"Not until we parked back at Rose Garden. And thank you very much for staying inside," she admitted for the first time.

Loretta raised both hands toward the ceiling. "Well, praise the Lord!"

"I knew it!" Kathleen beamed. "Was it a good kiss?"

"It made my knees weak," Sam answered.

"I need to tell him why I didn't tell you that he called and came by, I suppose." Kathleen sighed. "I just didn't feel like you needed any more on you at that time. And Noah needed to figure out just what he wanted after Laura left. I always liked the idea of y'all together, but timing is key in good love stories."

Sam topped another Club cracker with a thick slice of pepper jack. "You were right. And I'm sure that Noah will forgive you too."

Loretta had brought her knitting to the table and held it in her lap. She was making something from thick white, fuzzy yarn that could possibly be a blanket. She wore a crooked smile and didn't even look up as she worked on whatever it was. "I'm proud of you for closing the door to your past, Sam. That took courage and a lot of guts to confront Liza Beth and forgive her and Chase for what they did to you."

"It felt good once I got over the initial fear of running into Liza Beth. And she didn't look knocked up when we saw each other, so that might just be rumors. I didn't really look at her that well. I had tunnel vision at the time," Sam said.

"God answers prayers when you pray together." Loretta winked at Sam and then beamed at Kathleen.

"Y'all have been praying for me?" Sam looked from Kathleen to Loretta for the answer.

"Ever since you got here," Kathleen answered as she reached over and patted Sam's hand. "We knew you needed a place to heal from something. Prayers were just part of the package of free room and board."

Sam's eyes burned with unshed tears. "I can't thank either of you enough for all that you've done for me. I didn't always listen, and you still loved me. I was hardheaded, but you let me figure things out on my own. And then you caught me when I fell and needed you so badly. I don't deserve either of you."

Kathleen shook her head and pinched Sam's cheek softly. "You deserve the world, kid, and don't you ever think otherwise."

"You are ours now," Loretta spoke up. "We claim you as ours. We haven't done anything special, baby girl. We've just loved ya."

Overcome, Sam reached across the table to snag Loretta's hand and bumped into the white and pink antique vase on the table between them. The thing toppled, and Sam tried to catch it but missed. It fell in slow motion all the way to the floor and shattered into a million jagged pieces. Sam jumped up so fast that it made her dizzy. She tried to gather the flowers in one hand and mop up the water with her other, but couldn't seem to get anything done.

"Hey, Katty, it ain't dark out just yet, but I think Sam just went ahead and started the celebrations early," Loretta said as she raised her charger plate over her head and started to cackle. She pushed her little tea saucer of snacks to a safe spot in front of her and began to swing the china charger to and fro above her head.

Kathleen nodded and raised a matching charger over her head too. "One, two, three . . ."

A bash as loud as a shotgun's blast sounded as the two women tossed their plates down at the same time and let out peals of laughter.

"Good riddance," Loretta muttered as she dusted her hands off and grabbed another cracker.

Sam was as confused as Nibbler seemed to be when he came bounding up to the closed French doors leading from the dining room into the living area. He pawed and sniffed on the other side and yapped a warning.

"He's letting us know that he doesn't like our ritual and he's going to take over supervising our holiday." Kathleen giggled.

"Ritual?" Sam gawked at the shattered pieces scattered across the heart pine floors of the room. "Darlin' girl," Kathleen said, "you just stumbled into the oddest yearly ceremony that Loretta and I celebrate here at Rose Garden. It ain't nothing to fret about. That vase was doomed from the time we sat down at the table. I promise it makes sense if you know the whole story."

"This is the wackiest Fourth of July tradition I've ever heard of. I'm gonna want the whole story from the top, please."

Loretta nodded toward Kathleen. "I reckon it's time to bring her in, Kathleen. The whole breaking of the vase proves it. But it ain't my story to tell, it's yours."

"It's both our stories, Rhett. But I'll start." Kathleen took a heavy breath and leaned one elbow on the table and looked Sam right in the eyes.

"I was fourteen when my daddy said I could go out with Thurman the first time," Kathleen said. "I thought I was the luckiest girl in the world, that the best-looking boy in Homestead had asked me to the Valentine's Day dance at the school. Mama made me a pretty pink dress, fixed my hair, even got me new shoes earlier that winter. Thurman was a handsome cut of a man, and he knew how to act the perfect gentleman when he wanted to. He was lean and had his suits tailored down in Avinger by this old Italian man who used to make suits for the mob. He was sharp. He was a bit older than me too, I remember he brought me a corsage of white carnations that night. He won my parents over and then me too. We got married two months before my eighteenth birthday, and my parents gave us that little cabin out on the front end of the property."

"The hunting cabin? That place is pretty small. Where did Loretta stay?" Sam asked.

"Oh, honey, that was more than twenty years before I moved into the Rose Garden," Loretta said with an amused expression. "I was off making a mess of my own life before that. I didn't come to live here until we were both sixty years old."

"She didn't show up until I had wasted forty-three years," Kathleen said with a long sigh. "Time's just lost if you're living under the thumb of an abusive bastard."

"Thurman hit you?" Sam was shocked, not believing that Kathleen would ever put up with that kind of thing.

The dismissive way that Kathleen shrugged in response made her stomach clench. So, Thurman and Jack really were cut from the same cloth.

Loretta butted in before Kathleen could say another word. "Baby, there's more ways to abuse a woman than with fists. Thurman preferred throwing things. He was real good at lying and manipulating her. Hell, he gaslit me a few times, and I was living in the same house. The son of a bitch knew Kathleen's mama would have his ass if Kathleen showed any bruises, so he was particular about how and when he'd hurt her when Mama Scott was alive."

Kathleen picked up from there. "He liked mental games the most. He'd only get physical if he had drunk too much. That's why holidays that centered around drinking were always the more hellish ones. He liked to show me and his buddies he was the man of the house, even if I owned it and the land it sat on. His drinking picked up a few years into our marriage, and everything went to hell. My wedding vows said that I would obey him. He never let me forget it."

Sam made a mental note to herself: *Do not make that promise even if it is traditional.*

"November 29, 1965. That was the day I threw it back in his face and reminded him that he had vowed the same damn thing to me before my parents, the preacher, and even God. He had promised he would love and cherish me, and I told him I wanted a divorce on the grounds of adultery. Andrew was at his aunt Maude's house that night."

"And?" Sam asked.

"He broke all of the plates from our wedding dishes," Kathleen answered. "A few weeks later, I found out for absolute sure that he had been cheating on me for years. I broke the rest of the wedding set that had survived. He'd get angry and leave town for a few days, then come back chipper again and find some way to make me take him back. And the boys would be so happy when their daddy came back, I couldn't be angry for long, at least not in front of them. But then something would set Thurman off, and he'd go into another rage. I never knew which Thurman I got that day until it was too late."

Sam shivered, not just physically, but all the way into her soul.

"Were you still living at the cabin?"

"No, my mama had died and left the house to me, so we had moved into this house by then. Daddy moved to Georgia to be near his sisters and got married again to a woman from there. That all happened while I was pregnant with Bubba. Thurman was the golden child in my father's eyes, and he knew to hide his temper 'til Daddy moved away. After that, there was no one checking in on us that could really talk sense into Thurman when he got in one of his moods and it got bad. I spent more time sweeping up broken dishes than I spent washing them. I remember thinking that he could have at least thrown the dirty ones. But oh, no! He pulled them from the china cabinet, not the sink."

"Why did you stay? I mean, how in the world did you manage it?" Sam asked.

"I had nowhere to go. Daddy thought I was lying when I called to tell him what Thurman was doing. Thurman called all our friends and my own daddy and told them all I had postpartum and was going crazy. Anything I told anyone, including my pastor, my father, my friends, all went up in smoke because I had been deemed mentally unwell since Bubba's birth. The boys were too young to really understand what was happening in the house when everything was at its peak. I went to a lawyer after one bad bout, determined to divorce him. He said Thurman would be entitled to half of everything we had accumulated since marriage, meaning this house. I hated him too much to let him have what had been in my family for generations . . ." She paused long enough to eat a fistful of blueberries. "But I already told you that part."

"That was the year that she made this place into a bed-and-breakfast, and then the year after that, I moved in," Loretta added.

"Loretta helped me manage the bed-and-breakfast. She ran it while I tried to manipulate things so Thurman wouldn't sleep with my clientele. I barely kept myself together through that time."

"I learned how to fix Sheetrock pretty good," Loretta went on with the story.

She reminded Sam of a sticky-faced child who was thrilled to show an adult a new dance move or a poor bug in a jar.

"The bastard threw a toaster at me once. That toaster still worked afterward, but it took me two weeks to figure out how to fix that hole in the wall. He didn't like it that Kathleen started sassing back more after I moved in, and said I was the bad influence." Loretta rolled her eyes toward the ceiling. "Maybe I was. But he was an old rabid dog that needed to be put down. After what I saw and heard him do to Kathleen, I knew there wasn't any way out of it. Thurman's brother was the sheriff at the time, and he just . . ."

Kathleen laughed at the mention of her dead husband's brother. "Ah yes, the grand poohbah of the Good Ole Boys' Club of Homestead. Loretta and some of our mutual church friends had already called the cops on Thurman, but no report was officially filed by anyone in the sheriff's office."

"Did the sheriff not believe you, or did he just not want it to be true?" Sam asked.

The dismal answer to her question was foreshadowed by the slumping shift in Kathleen's shoulders. "He knew Thurman as well as I did. That was what tasted so bitter so many years afterward. He knew what I was up against, but"—she shrugged—"he was

Thurman's brother and drinking buddy. Having a relative accused of domestic violence, rape, and a handful of other felonies doesn't look too good when you got a reelection coming up in a few months. So, I was alone in it. I ain't proud of my actions back then, but I did what any wounded animal with its back in the corner does. I bared all my teeth and went berserk. I threatened to kill him if he touched me again. My hissy fit worked for a while. I threatened to burn the whole house down. He started taking women down to the hunting lodge and stopped bringing women to a bedroom here at the B&B."

Sam frowned. "The fact that the hunting lodge was his hookup shack makes Jack taking me there even grosser."

"So gross." Loretta shuddered.

Kathleen shivered at the same time. "One day when the boys were still little and in school, I was in the attic hiding out till Thurman finished his tirade and headed to the bar. While I was stuck up there, I went through a corner of the attic where my mother had left some chests and leather suitcases. I opened a hope chest full of quilts and petticoats and such. There were pillowcases and quilts and all sorts of things that men don't care to go through once a woman is dead. I even found a long black velvet overcoat that I remembered her wearing to funerals in the wintertime. I pulled it out and held it up to me, but it hung crooked, like it had a weight on one side. I felt all along and found her diary sewn into the pocket."

Sam hung on every word and when Kathleen paused, she asked, "Did you read it?"

"Yes, I did. It was an omen that I found it when I did. I sat in her old rocking chair that had a busted rung in the back and read until the boys came home from school. Every time I got a free minute, I stole a few hours and read more—mostly when the boys were in school or when Thurman and the kids were sleeping. I found out that my daddy and Thurman had been cut from the same cloth. Mama hid the uglier bits from me, just like I had done with the boys. I think a lot of women did that back then because image was everything for the family's reputation. And being a divorced woman was too big of a scandal to pass to your kids. So, she had stuck it out. Daddy was the pot. No wonder he always vouched for the kettle." Kathleen's pained expression said more than her words.

"I need a beer." Kathleen stood and walked to the fridge unceremoniously as Loretta continued rambling for her.

"Thurman died the next summer on July Fourth, so we celebrate the old devil passing on by breaking dishes we have chipped in the year past. We start anew and call it our own New Year's Day. You just helped us bring in another Rose Garden New Year by breaking that vase, honey. I thought it was hideous anyhow."

"Rhett, you said you liked it when I bought it!" Kathleen protested.

"I lied." Loretta's face lit up in a gleeful grin. "Sam, you probably need to get ready. The eager dog that Noah is, there's no doubt that he will get here early to pick you up."

Kathleen shooed Sam with a flick of her wrist. "Speaking of eager dogs, make sure to bring Nibbler to your room. Rhett and I will clean up the festivities a little later. I have a few more I may wanna add to the floor gallery before I finish this beer. I'll snuggle Nibbler when the real fireworks start, so don't worry."

"Wear that little red cotton dress you have in the closet. It will keep you cool and still be festive. Oh! And pair it with your brown flats!" Loretta said.

Sam had never—from day one—seen Kathleen and Loretta the way that Jack had described them when he told her about them.

Eccentric was a word Sam heard often in town. But her description of the two was bold, independent, self-sufficient, encouraging, and hilarious. Certainly not eccentric. But in moments like this, when Kathleen, wearing her signature overalls, chucked a teacup on the ground like a football after a winning touchdown and took another swig of Corona, Sam mentally added maybe a smidgen of eccentric to the list of reasons why she loved these women. And then Loretta hiked a hip and perched like a bird, knocking a chipped martini glass from the edge of the table as Kathleen tossed a bowl next. Oh, yes, Sam could finally see how the word "eccentric" could fit into an apt description of them.

They're perfect for you, Inez whispered with an almost audible giggle.

I agree, Inez, Sam said silently.

Kathleen pointed at Sam. "Go on, get a move on, missy, or Loretta is gonna come up there and dress you. I can't hold her back forever."

It had been a very long time since someone had tried to dress Sam for an event. Maybe the second set of mothers that Madam Fate gave her didn't realize she was thirty years old. They had only had her for a few months, so she was still a baby to them.

Even though the night was still with no breeze and the heat was almost unbearable, Sam sat close to Noah in the football stands. The first bursts of red, white, and blue sparkles brought thoughts of childhood to mind for her, the faded grass field stretched out ahead of them in a dark silent blob as the fireworks shot and screamed above the tree line.

"It's beautiful," she whispered.

Noah gazed at her. "You're beautiful."

She met his eyes and leaned closer to him. "Thank you."

He softly pressed his lips to hers as the fireworks continued to pop off in the distance. His hand rested softly over her ear and muffled the loud sounds. After a few minutes, it moved to her neck to pull her closer. They stayed like that, and the whole world spun around them. Sam felt like she was a pin on the globe and a drunk giant had just slapped that globe into motion. It was all she could do to hold on to Noah and not get shot off into space as the world spun around her. Her body hummed with a feminine ache she hadn't felt with such ferocity in a long time. When he kissed her again, she gripped the bleacher below her and tried to remember to breathe.

When the last big display of the grand finale had sputtered out, Noah draped his arm back around Sam's shoulders, and tingles danced down her spine. Their one agreement in moving forward was to take things slow. Noah said he wanted *to do this right*, but Sam had wanted to rip his clothes off by the end of June. She understood their situation called for a slow burn, but every one of his touches and kisses were so hot that it took every bit of her self-control to not rush things.

Sam was living a romance novel currently, so there was little need to read about other folks' happily ever afters. One night over wine and chocolate cake, he finally admitted that he had read all the books she had raved about, backing his claim up as she gawked at him. "I just needed to know what it was that you wanted in your love story," he said.

That admission sent her hormones into overdrive, but then she thought about all the raunchier Harlequin romances that she raved on about that had blisteringly scandalous sex scenes in between their covers.

If he had read them, well then, he'll be very well trained on what you like. Inez was in her head as quick as a whip. Sam felt her whole body fused and warm to the color of her dress as they started walking back to Noah's car May.

"Hey, y'all!" Kara's drawl was thick as she hollered from the gate. "Look what I got for my birthday. I found myself a real cowboy."

Kara made her way over to them with her arm looped in the arm of a blue-eyed cowboy with the Carhartt jacket, hat, and boots to prove it. "This is Danny. Danny, this here is Samantha and this is Noah."

The blond-haired guy shook both of their hands and murmured hellos as Kara continued, "We met when I was on a girls' trip to Linden in between trips to see my mama, and we two-stepped all night and went on a date the next night. He's a rancher from up north and just sold his last group of steers, so he's visiting me and meeting everybody. I wanted to show him our old high school with all the fireworks, but I guess we're too late!"

Sam had never seen Kara smile so big before. The girl positively beamed at the man beside her, and there was no doubt the fireworks were the last thing she cared about.

"Y'all look cute together." Sam smiled. "I'm glad you found each other. And it's good to officially meet you, Danny. Welcome to Homestead!"

Danny tipped his hat as Kara carried on for him.

"Me too, it's a dream come true. We both want a farm and our own cattle one day. He says he wants six kids, but I told him I'd start with two, and we could go from there." Kara laughed and waved over her shoulder as she and the cowboy headed out of the hometown stadium.

Sam stared at Noah. "How many kids do you want, Noah?"

"How many kids do you want?"

"Three, I think. Maybe just two."

"Three is a great number. It's my favorite number, actually."

207

"Are you just saying that?"

"No, I mean it."

"What if I had said I wanted fifteen children?"

"Well that would have been crazy, because fifteen is my second favorite number." His smile continued to grow. "If that's really what you want, we'd have to start working on that pretty soon though."

"They say practice makes perfect," Sam whispered.

Noah's eyes glowed amber at the cheeky response from Sam, and he looked like he might just pounce on her right then.

"Would you want a five-bedroom house one day, like your parents have?" Noah asked.

That question seemed to come out of left field, but Sam shook her head. "I don't know. I want space to have family and friends over. I want a place to call my own and raise my kids, somewhere they'll always have to come back home to. It doesn't matter how many bedrooms. The important thing to me is that my family can be together under one roof. That's what I want. And a garden! I want a garden out back of the kitchen."

"I think that sounds like the perfect home," Noah whispered.

"Should I ask what you're thinking about?"

"It'll be better as a surprise," he assured her. "For tonight though, do you wanna go back to the Rose Garden, the speakeasy, or my trailer?"

"Trailer please. I want some raspberry tea, and I left it at your place the other day. Also, I'd like for us to hang out for a bit before I need to head back to Rose Garden."

She noticed that Noah drove fifteen miles over the speed limit all the way through town.

CHAPTER THIRTEEN

BED OF ROSES

It had taken a full year of dreaming and dating and erasing and resketching before Sam and Noah had the blueprints for the house of their dreams completed and were finally ready to break ground.

Noah bought Thurman's old hunting lodge and the eighty-six acres surrounding it from Kathleen. When the backhoes came on site that morning, he called Kathleen and Sam and asked the crew to take an early lunch break. He handed one of the foreman a wad of cash to buy everyone's food. Then he grabbed three hard hats from the back of his truck.

When the three women appeared at the cabin, he handed Sam one of the hard hats and motioned toward the backhoe.

"Oh, no!" Sam shook her head. "Kathleen should get to take the first swings at the place. She's the one who needs to bash this place into smithereens. It's overdue."

Sam could sense she was witnessing something special as she held Noah's hand and watched with a whoop and a holler as

Kathleen bashed through the roof of the living room with the giant metal bucket. Her history with the little cabin ran deeper than Sam's one dark memory of it, and Sam was getting to watch her dismantle her past pain. Loose strands of her hair bounced around under her hard hat as she abolished Thurman's mark on the property—once and for all.

Most of the rubble was hauled off later that afternoon, and Kathleen and Sam stared at the clearing where the cabin used to be. The place that Sam avoided and Kathleen despised. Sam was pretty sure that Kathleen had experienced a cathartic moment that afternoon just like she did.

With the cabin gone, a trailer brought in a load of rebar to begin the new foundation. Sam and Noah were planting a new seed of a dream with this project. A new dream that would rise like a phoenix soon enough from the past ashes of pain.

With Loretta and Kathleen's help, Sam planned to plant wild-flowers down the new driveway and find a mailbox real soon. She was ready for a life with Noah in their two-story cottage settled back in the woods, she was ready to fill the meadow with the love and memories it deserved.

Noah hadn't asked Sam to marry him, but as the summer had come to an end, he began asking her more pointed questions about diamonds and ring sizes during casual conversation. She had been focused on the house designs, deriving incredible amounts of joy from deciding where they'd put the fridge and how many rooms they felt they may need over time.

She had forgotten they had almost skipped a whole step. He was talking about carats, and her thoughts were more concerned with where the nursery should be. Noah was the love of her life, and he was wholly and completely hers. She felt that in every cell of her body. No ring, no matter how big, no matter what kind or cut or color, would change that. But one evening after they'd been out to check on the progress of the house, he had that look on his face again.

"What kind of ring would you like to have?"

She stopped thinking about nurseries and looked up into his warm brown eyes. "Anything you pick will be exactly what I've wanted. Size eight. That is, if you're asking about what I think you are."

When his face flushed, the freckles across his nose darkened. He drew her into his arms and hugged her tightly. "So, size eight?"

"That's right." She snuggled down close to his chest.

Her phone buzzed, and she knew without even pulling it from her pocket that it was her mama. "Hey, I'm gonna answer this real quick. I want to ask Mama's advice on the tile for the powder room and see if she had a suggestion on what type of siding we should use. I think she'll agree with us on the dark green tile for the powder room, but I don't know what color to go with for the appliances, and I wanna think it through before we order any tile."

"Of course," Noah agreed. "Go ahead and answer and get her opinion, I like the green tile idea. I'm just gonna go mark off some areas I want to build around your garden. I think raised garden beds would be nice around the edges of the main plot and your herb garden." This man knew exactly how to talk to a woman.

"I love you, Noah Carter," she murmured.

"I love you more," he teased and kissed her on the forehead. "Now talk to your mama and get her opinion on tile and paint."

She pulled her phone from the pocket of her jeans, answered, and spared no time going into talk of paint swatches and tile design.

Finally, Wanette got a word in edgewise. "Baby, however you decorate this house, that's how it should be. Your love is what will make this house a home. Not paint colors or fancy tile. Right now, I gotta let you go. I'm expecting company tomorrow afternoon, and I gotta get a cheesecake made up."

"Cheesecake? Without me? That's cruel, Mama." Sam sighed.

"Well, come home, and I'll make you one," Wanette said cheekily.

"Okay, then. We'll visit soon, I promise!" Sam said. "I think I'm going to go with the dark green tile. I love you, call me after your company leaves tomorrow."

Her mama ended the call, and Sam tucked her phone back in her pocket. She stood in the middle of where she supposed the tiny, unfinished powder room would be and let her mind wander. Noah had thought of everything up to and including putting a satellite out behind Kathleen's house to give them all better service on the hill. She sent another little prayer of thanks up to God for sending her the right man when she was ready for him.

"Thank you, for making my car break down when you did," she whispered.

That night, Samantha was almost asleep when a gentle knock at her bedroom door brought her into a sitting position and Kathleen popped her head inside. "I hope I didn't wake you, but Noah left something for you on the kitchen counter. You should come on downstairs and see it."

Sam came out of her room in her pajama bottoms and a faded, oversized T-shirt.

"Put some damn pants on, not in your pajamas, girl!" Loretta shouted.

"Yes, ma'am," Sam shot back.

She went back to her room, threw on jeans, and slipped her feet into tennis shoes. Then she buttoned one of Noah's long-sleeved thinner flannel shirts up. She made her way down the stairs and to the kitchen. Her flashlight, well, *his* flashlight was sitting on the counter, acting as a paperweight for a note underneath.

Come see what our love has been building. Don't forget your flashlight this time. —Noah

Sam stuffed the note in her front pocket and took off toward the old cabin site with the flashlight in hand. She called out her goodbyes over her shoulder with Nibbler following fast behind her. She knew what Noah had meant by what their love had been building. He had said the day before that the concrete would probably be cured by today. The foundation for their new home was almost done. That meant they were one step closer to their forever.

She stopped and gasped when she came into the clearing. Noah had strung lights up over every corner of the fresh cement, now standing solid. A blanket lay in the middle of the foundation of their future home, and wine and bread popped out of the top of a picnic basket nearby.

"What are you doing?"

"I'm building a life with you, Sam." Noah held his arms out wide. "Damn, that feels good to say. Our cornerstone is ready, the cement has finally cured, and I wanted to celebrate this first step with you."

She clicked off the flashlight and ran across the concrete pad, wrapped her arms around him, and rose onto her tiptoes to kiss him—long, lingering, and passionately. He picked her up and spun her around as they continued kissing until Noah set her back on her feet.

"This is everything I could've ever wanted, Noah. I can't wait to make a house into a home with you."

"Me too, Sam," he said. "I put the house in your name. And the land."

"You did what?" Had she heard him right? Surely not.

"And May too. She should be yours now."

"You're giving me the house? And May?" Sam gasped.

"Yeah, I am. You deserve a piece of Homestead that is truly yours to call home. The house was always going to be in your name. I'll just get to live here with you if you'll have me." Noah locked eyes with her. "But as far as May goes, think of her as an early wedding gift."

"A wedding gift?"

"Marry me, Sam. You'd make me the happiest man in the world if you'd marry me."

"Yes," she answered. "Forever, yes!"

Loretta eyed the ring on Sam's left hand over coffee the next morning. "I'm surprised you didn't have to resize it."

"Isn't it beautiful?" Sam said with a sigh. "I can't believe he gave me his mother's engagement ring."

Kathleen picked up Sam's finger and touched the ring. "Mrs. Carter's old ring fitting your finger like Cinderella's glass slipper. Now that's the Lord's work."

"I still can't believe he planned all this," Sam said and blushed at what had happened after he put the ring on her finger.

They started making out on the blanket, but then after a few minutes, he stood up and pretended to close a door. "What goes on in our bedroom is our business and not the rest of the world's."

They had made sweet, sweet love right there where their bedroom would be—smack dab on the cement slab. Afterward, they went to the trailer and made love again before falling asleep in each other's arms. That morning, Sam was still a bit loopy from equal parts of low sleep as well as the high around a new engagement when Noah dropped her off at the B&B.

"There's another surprise," Kathleen said.

"What?" Sam asked.

"Loretta packed a go bag for you," Kathleen said. "And I whipped up a go bag of breakfast and snacks for you. Noah will be here soon with May. He called your mama and daddy yesterday to plan a trip to Rosepine to see your family and tell them about your engagement. Your sisters will be there. Noah thought of everything."

"Vivian is able to step back in at the florist shop while you're gone, honey." Loretta squeezed her arm, and the old gals walked her to the car. "Go enjoy yourself, then y'all can get back and be all in love! Go have your time in the sun. We got the Nibble Monster."

Noah opened her door as the two women hugged her again.

"We'll throw you two a little bash here in Homestead when you get back. How does that sound?" Kathleen asked.

"If it's not too much of a hassle, that would be really special, Kathleen, and thank you," Noah answered for both of them.

Sam nodded vigorously and hugged the woman again before finally settling into the passenger seat. "I don't know when we'll be back since he's keeping everything a secret right now, so I guess I'll just see you when I see you."

Loretta looked at Kathleen and remarked, "He didn't tell her what else he has planned yet?" To which Kathleen responded with a solid thwack to Loretta's shoulder.

"Should I be worried?" Sam asked as she looked into his eyes.

"Nope, just happy." He brought her hand to his lips and kissed her knuckles and then pulled out of the Rose Garden lane.

Sam couldn't seem to wipe the aggravating sweaty piece of hair from her face without rubbing dirt all over herself, and she finally sat back on her heels to yank off her gloves and scrub at her face with both hands. She'd asked Kathleen to help her graft some of the roses so she could grow them along the lane to her new home that had been finished a week before they had married in a simple ceremony in her folks' backyard.

Kathleen had seemed hesitant at first, but Sam had begged and pleaded.

"They remind me of you, and that's what first drew me here. Please, Kathleen. I'll do the work if you just show me how."

So, on a spring morning as the sun crested over the white pines and the dew had dried, Sam and Kathleen collected large cuttings off most of the roses around the Rose Garden. They had lined up most of them, all now soaking in buckets of water when they took their first break on the back porch. They sipped cold ice water in silence as the midday sun on the shady grove around the house peeked in and out from behind big, fluffy white clouds.

Sam gazed out at the dense tree line in the far back of the clearing. "When did you plant these gorgeous red roses?"

"I didn't plant these roses."

"What do you mean?"

"I planted Ducher roses, Sam."

"But, aren't they . . ."

"Yes, they are." Kathleen's eyes dropped to the wooden step below her booted toes. When she looked back up at Sam, her expression had aged her twenty years. "I should have told you a long time ago, but I worried about what you would think of me, but I-I do regret what I did, at least some of the time."

"Ooookay . . ." Sam said slowly and set her glass over near the water pitcher. "Is this something juicy?"

"I've made it right with God, at least as much as I could on this matter. He knows I would've taken it back once it was over if I could have, but I couldn't by then. I may burn in hell one day for my actions, but I just couldn't handle Thurman's abuse any longer. I had to get out, Sam. And at that point, I saw no other way to stop the torment than just ending it."

"Did you try to hurt yourself?" Sam asked.

"It was either me or him," Kathleen answered. "Life is a bed, Sam. You decide when you wake up each morning. You decide who you let in it. You decide if you get drunk and piss on it. I was just too young and didn't know no better. I picked the wrong bed to lie down on. So, when Thurman was running around and I knew I couldn't leave him, I just went outside. Not outside the marriage, mind you, but to gardening. Mama helped me plant the first few rows, then I went overboard. I planted roses in all corners of the fence around the property, and while my husband was tending to women around town and in other cities, I tended them roses. His mama had told him that real southern ladies always have a rose garden, and something in me kept whispering that if I could be just how he would like me, he wouldn't run away anymore. If I was a better woman, he wouldn't hurt me. He would be happy and stay at home. I clung to that idea and treated this garden like it was my full-time job once the boys were in high school and driving themselves. I needed to love something, to tend to something. And Thurman had started pulling the boys away from me when they were old enough to go hunting with him."

"That must have been hell to get through," Sam muttered.

"We didn't always have awful times. He liked that I kept the yard neat and tidy and seemed appreciative when he'd throw one of his parties. He could be the life of the party during those times. But every time, at some point in a long night, something would go amiss. A button would be missing from one of his shirts. A rose bush would dare to lose its blooms the day before guests arrived, hell, I'd track dirt in through the back door on a Sunday. Anything he didn't like was treated as a direct blow against him."

She paused.

Sam gave her time, and after a while she went on. "He yanked me around so bad that I thought he broke my shoulder after the barbecue we threw the weekend before Independence Day one year. Loretta came in that night, popped my shoulder back into place, and wrapped it up for me. I begged her not to tell anyone, and she didn't. Instead, she put me to bed and slipped back outside before Thurman came in. The next morning, she was standing by my bed nudging my shoulder until I woke up. She had her hand over my mouth to keep me from squealing. We left Thurman sleeping, and I followed her into the woods. Since we were kids, Loretta's granddaddy had been known as a medicine man. Sounds funny if you'd never seen it, but he could blow a burn right off someone's fingers, and he could pray thrush from a child. He could heal folks. But he also knew how to kill folks. He had taught Loretta as a little girl how to gather in the woods for his tinctures and such. He had taught her what helped and what hurt."

Kathleen paused here and put her arm around her knees and rocked a bit on the step she sat on. "Thurman was getting worse and worse. He had pulled a gun out the last time I made him mad. I had told him I was going to leave him, and I'd made up my mind. He went and got his gun out of his truck and held me down. He told me he'd kill the boys if I left him. He said he'd take his shotgun and he'd track both my boys down, shoot them, and then he would come back and kill me. He said he'd take what I loved most before he'd end it. And I believed him."

"She didn't want to do anything to him, but I talked her into it. I'm the one who showed her how." Loretta's stoic voice came from the doorway behind them.

She walked out and sat on the steps, picking at the chipping paint with one of her long fingernails. "He would've killed Kathleen. I'd seen what Thurman could be like when he got in one of his fits. I'd seen him nearly kill a dog for pissing inside. And he loved that dog."

"How did you do it?" Sam whispered.

"We just celebrated the Fourth of July as usual," Kathleen answered.

"Yep, all of his favorites," Loretta said with a nod. "Ham, creamed corn, black-eyed peas, banana pudding, the works."

"His favorite dessert was a buttermilk almond pound cake I'd make with a heavy almond glaze. That and lime pound cake. He liked a lot of lime and extra almond extract. So that's what we made for him," Kathleen said.

"We were as heavy-handed as he normally liked it," Loretta added. "He ate three slices, two of the almond and a thick one of the lime. He got too full to get drunk and fell asleep in his chair in his room in front of the television. We found him cold the next morning and called the sheriff. A new one that wasn't kin to him."

"The coroner didn't rat y'all out?"

"The coroner was an old friend and just happened to be one of the women who had called the cops on Thurman twenty years before and had been ignored back then. She agreed with Loretta that no autopsy was needed and declared that it was clearly a heart attack. She owned the funeral home and took care of the cremation for us too."

"What did you do with the ashes?" Sam asked.

"I killed my husband. Samantha, I baked him two cakes, either one of which could make his heart stop, and you're wondering if I kept his ashes?" Kathleen gasped, but Loretta laughed.

"A mean enough man is cruelest to the ones closest, and some folks ain't worth all the second chances they get," Sam simply parroted back the wisdom Loretta had passed on.

Loretta chuckled. "A new employee at the funeral home tried to talk her into a fancy vase and even asked if she wanted one that they called the companion urn. Since she and Thurman had been married so long, he reckoned they might want to be together in death."

"I'd rather sell ice cream to Eskimos for eternity." Kathleen's tone had a sharp edge to it, but then softened. "Loretta and I will be buried in my family's plot north of town—side by side. Our joint tombstone is already engraved with everything but our death dates."

Sam let out a deep breath and leaned back on the step behind her. "Well, what did you do with him, then? Is he just tucked back in a closet somewhere in Rose Garden now with last year's Christmas decorations?"

"No, honey," Loretta answered. "We took that cheap cardboard box full of his ashes out to the compost pile and chunked him in with the rest of the garbage that we'd throwed out there."

"Then we tossed in the box too and raked it all up and spit on it for good measure." Kathleen smiled at the memory. "That winter when the last rose died, I pruned them back clear to the dirt and used the compost to fertilize them. When I finished, I told him that his ghost could keep his roses alive."

"He liked them more than you did?" Sam asked.

"Not at all, but it was another thing he could bitch at me about. I wanted everything that made me think of him to pass on with him."

"The roses took us giving them Thurman's old, poisoned compost very personally and grew back with a vendetta the next year. They all looked dead as doornails until spring and then bam!" Loretta threw her arms back dramatically for emphasis. "Them damn roses came back bigger and bigger than ever before, and we could barely keep a handle on them from then on. Spooky, huh?"

"Maybe his ashes had some wild blood in them." Sam chuckled.

"I'm sure they did." Loretta laughed.

"I based the Rose Petal off the sheer demand for the roses that started growing that year. Seems like no one could find a deeper red rose with so big of a bloom anywhere in the Bible Belt. The roses practically keep the flower shop and the Rose Garden open by themselves."

"I guess that's a Ducher rose for you," Sam tossed back at Kathleen with a smile.

"These aren't Ducher roses. My mama and I planted Duchers on this land. And I know it because it was the only kind she wanted to grow. These roses might look like this now." Kathleen pulled her pocketknife from the front pocket of her overalls and cut a bloom off the bush beside her, twirling the bloodred petals in between her fingers. "But the only roses I've ever planted here were snow white."

RECIPES

Dear Readers,

Kathleen is very particular about who gets her recipes, but she gave us permission to include her buttermilk almond pound cake and lime pound cake recipes in this story.

We hope you enjoy them!

Buttermilk Almond Pound Cake

<u>For the cake batter:</u>

½ cup butter, softened

1 cup sugar

3 large eggs

1 ½ cups cake flour, sifted

Pinch of salt

½ cup buttermilk

¼ teaspoon baking soda

½ teaspoon vanilla extract

2 teaspoons almond extract

1. Preheat the oven to 350 degrees F.
2. Grease and flour a standard-size loaf pan. Kathleen likes to use sugar instead of flour.
3. In a mixing bowl, beat the butter until creamy and add the sugar a little at a time until it is fully incorporated. Then add the eggs one at a time, beating only until the yellow disappears after each egg.

4. Measure the flour, then sift it and the salt together into a separate bowl.

5. Shake the container of buttermilk to mix it well. Then pour it into a glass measuring cup. Add the baking soda and stir to dissolve. The mixture will rise as a reaction takes place between the buttermilk and baking soda.

6. Alternate adding the flour and buttermilk to the batter, starting and ending with flour. Beat at a low speed after each addition, being careful not to overbeat.

7. Stir in the vanilla and almond extracts.

8. Pour the batter into the prepared pan.

9. Bake for 55–60 minutes or until an inserted toothpick comes out clean. If the top of the cake is getting too brown, add a greased sheet of aluminum foil to the top of the cake.

10. After removing the baked cake from the oven, let it sit for 5 minutes to cool. Then run a knife around the edges and carefully turn it out onto a wire rack and let it finish cooling.

For the syrup:

1. Boil 2 tablespoons water and 2 tablespoons sugar together until the sugar is melted.

2. Add 1 teaspoon almond extract.

3. When the cake is cooled, use a brush to paint the syrup onto the cake, covering the top and sides until all the mixture is used.

For the glaze:

1. Mix together 1 tablespoon water, 2 teaspoons almond extract, and 1 cup powdered sugar, adding a drop or two of water at a time to make a smooth glaze.

2. Drizzle on top of the cake!

Lime Pound Cake

<u>For the cake batter:</u>

½ cup butter, softened

1 ¼ cups sugar

3 eggs

1 ¾ cups cake flour

½ cup buttermilk

¼ teaspoon soda

2 tablespoons lime juice

1 tablespoon Limoncello (or replace with 1 tablespoon lime juice)

1. Preheat the oven to 350 degrees F.
2. Grease and flour a standard size loaf pan. Kathleen likes to use sugar instead of flour.
3. In a mixing bowl, beat the butter until creamy and add the sugar a little at a time until it is fully incorporated. Beat about 5 minutes.
4. Add the eggs one at a time, beating only until the yellow disappears after each egg.
5. Measure out the flour and then sift it and the salt together into a separate bowl.
6. Shake the container of buttermilk to mix it well. Then pour it into a glass measuring cup. Add the baking soda and stir to dissolve. The mixture will rise as a reaction takes place between the buttermilk and baking soda.
7. Alternate adding the flour and buttermilk to the batter, starting and ending with flour. Beat at a low speed after each addition, being careful not to overbeat.
8. Stir in the lime juice and Limoncello if using.
9. Pour the batter into the prepared pan.

10. Bake for 55–60 minutes or until an inserted toothpick comes out clean. If the top of the cake is getting too brown, add a greased sheet of aluminum foil to the top of the cake.
11. After removing the baked cake from the oven, let it sit for 5 minutes to cool. Then run a knife around the edges and carefully turn it out onto a wire rack and let it finish cooling.

For the syrup:
1. Boil 2 tablespoons water and 2 tablespoons sugar together until the sugar is melted.
2. Add 1 teaspoon lime juice.
3. When the cake is cooled, use a brush to paint the syrup onto the cake, covering the top and sides and painting until all the mixture is used.

For the glaze:
1. Mix together 1 tablespoon water, 3 tablespoons lime juice or a mixture of lime juice and Limoncello, and 1 cup powdered sugar.
2. Add a drop or two of water at a time to make the glaze smooth.
3. Drizzle on top of the cake!

ABOUT THE AUTHORS

Caylee Hammack is a country singer, songwriter, and producer signed with Capitol Records Nashville. A corecipient, with Miranda Lambert, of the Academy of Country Music's "Music Event of the Year" honor, she has been identified as an "Artist to Watch" by *The Bobby Bones Show*, *Rolling Stone*, and *Hits* magazine. Her debut album, *If It Wasn't for You*, earned high praise from critics, with her deeply personal song "Small Town Hypocrite" named a "Best Song of 2020" by NPR and *Esquire*. Her sophomore album, *Bed of Roses*, is a sonic storybook of the tales and characters that shaped her into who she is today.

With the help of her close friends and creatives, including John Osborne of the Brothers Osborne, Hammack has tended the garden of her life and fostered her most authentic sound, harnessing the power of raw storytelling that has set her apart as an artist. For more information, visit www.cayleehammack.com.

Carolyn Brown is the *New York Times–*, *USA Today–*, *Wall Street Journal–*, and *Washington Post–*bestselling author of more than a hundred novels and several novellas. A recipient of the Booksellers' Best Award and the Montlake Diamond Award as well as a three-time recipient of the National Readers' Choice Award, her work has been published for more than twenty years, and her books have been translated into twenty-one languages. When she's not writing, Brown enjoys plotting new stories on road trips with her family. To learn more visit www.carolynbrownbooks.com.

A STORY IN EVERY LYRIC,
A SONG ON EVERY PAGE.

LISTEN TO THE ALBUM IN REVERSE ORDER
TO COINCIDE WITH THE CHAPTERS
OF THE BOOK!

ALBUM AND AUDIOBOOK
AVAILABLE WHEREVER YOU LISTEN

CONNECT WITH

NEW YORK TIMES & USA TODAY
BESTSELLING AUTHOR

CAROLYN BROWN

CAROLYNBROWNBOOKS.COM

FOR A GOOD TIME

follow us on our socials

 podiumentertainment.com

 @podiumentertainment

 /podiumentertainment

 @podium_ent

 @podiumentertainment